Summer Guest
by
Sylvia Melvin

Sylvia (Sally) Melvin

This is a work of fiction. Names, characters, places and events are products of the author's imagination or are used fictitiously. Any resemblance to actual persons, living or dead, locales or events is entirely coincidental.

This book is dedicated to my parents, Harry and Jennie Matthews. Their hard work and devotion to Pine Lake Lodge inspired the writing of this novel.

Chapter One

"It isn't fair! They're going to ruin us!"

"I don't like the situation either."

Henry Lawrence picked up a maul and whacked the top of a two-by-four stake into the loose, brown soil. "I resent how oil companies and some cartel thousands of miles from Ontario can complicate our lives."

"Daddy, I paid six-dollars a liter to fill up my car last week! That's pure robbery, plain and simple!"

"They don't care. That's why the Americans can't afford to travel to our neck of the woods. "We've never had so many cancellations. Not in thirty-five years."

"We're looking at some hard times, aren't we?"

"Time to face the facts, Amy. Business is bad. And not just for us. Saw Andy McDonald in town yesterday. Said he had to lay off his best guide.

"Whip-poor-will Lodge?"

"Yep. Been with him ten years. The tourist industry's takin' a beating. Especially the fishing lodges."

1

Her father, still lean and strong at sixty, balding, with a lined, weather-beaten face, gave the stake one last strike before he picked up a piece of plywood. "Never thought I'd be puttin' up a 'For Sale' sign but it's our only hope. Henry dropped his head. "I dread telling your mother it's come to this, knowing how much she's suffered already."

Henry's words pierced his daughter's heart.

"Daddy, I know how much you miss and love her-- how tough it's been on you."

"The two years have been hard on you, too. Not easy for a girl with her mother in a psychiatric ward. I've been proud of the way you've handle the responsibilities around here."

"She taught me well. I've learned a little in my twenty-four years. I can handle it."

Amy felt a mixture of anger and sadness as she surveyed the only home she'd ever known. Built of logs hewn by hand, it sat on a gentle slope overlooking a lake eight miles long and a half mile wide. On either side of the lodge, spruce and pine trees sheltered smaller cabins. A boathouse with a wooden ramp stretched down to the sandy beach at the east end of the property. Since the lodge was accessible only by boat, no other motor vehicles interrupted the peaceful privacy coveted by its patrons.

From the time she was a child, the deep, clear water filled with aquatic plants and animals lured Amy to its hidden depths. Her nostrils tingled at its scent: a mixture of sweet-smelling grasses, white and yellow water lilies, fish, tadpoles, clams and mud. She could hear the waves lap against the water-logged planks of the old dock. Often the rhythm of their movement caressed her troubled mind.

Today was different. The investment of labor her parents sowed into the land they loved was on the verge of jeopardy, and thought of leaving cast an unwelcome shadow on their lives. Her eyes skimmed the surface of the lake. In the distance, a young skier circled a forested island behind a shiny speedboat. Nearby, a smaller boat sat anchored beside a bed of lily pads with its lone occupant anticipating a jerk and bend of his pole. Children jumped and splashed as small waves chased them to the sandy beach. On the surface, life here appeared to be normal, but an undercurrent of fear and an uncertain future held Amy's thoughts hostage.

There was a gentle breeze and she pushed back auburn hair that danced around her ears and freckled face. The distant purr of an approaching outboard motor caught her attention and green eyes, serious beyond her years, squinted against the glare of the four o'clock sun.

"We've got company." She strained to see if she could recognize who it was.

Henry put down the maul and turned to investigate. "Looks like one of the Harper boys from the marina."

The boat came closer. "It's Ted all right. There's no mistaking that red hair. I wonder who he has with him? It better not be that real estate agent pestering me about a listing again. I told him I've run this place successfully for thirty-five years and I'm not letting some city slicker tell me what to do."

"Can't blame you."

"Told me he has all kinds of contacts. My way might take a little longer, but I want to know who I'm selling to."

"Just let me put my two cents worth in and we'll have him out of here in no time," suggested Amy.

Ted cut the motor's throttle and called out, "Hey, Amy, catch the bow, will you?"

She ran down to the edge of the dock just as the stranger threw her the rope. The boat hit a plank with a thud, knocking both men off balance.

"Nice try, sweetheart," laughed Ted. "Brought you a guest from Ohio. Think you can put him up for a while?"

It was Ted's nature to tease about something serious. He knew there'd been vacant cottages most of the summer.

This energy fiasco hurt his marina business, too.

"No problem. We're open for business." Amy beckoned to her father to come down to the dock.

"I'm Henry Lawrence and this is my daughter, Amy." Henry wasted no time in welcoming the stranger. The men exchanged handshakes and Amy nodded with a welcoming smile.

"Matt Monroe. Pleased to meet you. I hear the fishing is pretty decent up here in northern Ontario."

"You've come to the right place," Henry affirmed.

"The walleye are hungry and the bass are taking just about anything you cast at them."

"I'm looking for quiet time, too,"

Henry was quick to pick up on his implication. "No need to worry. No one will bother you."

"Cabin eight is private," She pointed to a log structure nestled in the pines at the end of the trail. "I'm sure you'll find it comfortable. Benny will come and carry your things."

While Henry went to find Benny, their chore-boy, and Ted secured the boat, Matt began unloading a piece of leather luggage, a box of groceries and his fishing gear. As he placed two rods on the dock, Amy commented, "You shouldn't have any problems landing a walleye with this equipment. Shakespeare's a good reel. We have a few ourselves."

"Sounds like you're a bit of an expert."

Ted interrupted before Amy could respond. "Who? Amy? She's one of the best. Born with a rod in one hand and a net in the other."

"Hmm, sounds like I should hire you to be my guide, Amy. A female guide--now that might be interesting. What do you say?"

Amy's face, already pink from the day's sun, flushed as she looked into the bluest eyes she'd ever seen. "Whoa!" she thought. "Where's this guy coming from? Sounds like 'attitude' to me." In a matter of minutes he'd managed to put her on the defensive.

His towering, well-toned, muscular frame capped with hair the color of ripe grain instantly recalled an image she'd spent the last four months trying to forget. The physical likeness to her ex-fiancé was uncanny, and Matt's patronizing tone revived her scarred, raw emotions.

Eric never could understand her love of the north and constantly made fun of her 'country ways'. They'd met during her senior year at university. He was in his last semester of law school and she was starting her Master's degree in education. His smooth talk and sophisticated manner was intoxicating. He courted her in flamboyant style and before the year was up she'd fallen in love.

It wasn't until after the engagement Amy sensed a change in their relationship. No matter how she tried to please him, he'd find fault. He criticized her clothes, her hair style, any weight gain, and even her friends.

The day he stated, "Your mother's nervous collapse is all in her head. She needs to get a grip," was the final curtain. Through tears of anger, Amy told him the marriage was off. She respected herself too much to tolerate his condescending treatment.

Before Amy had time to say anything else to Matt, Benny, a lanky lad of fourteen, dressed in jeans, a dirty tee-shirt, and a baseball cap came running up to them.

"Benny, this is Mr. Monroe. Take his things to cabin eight." Her brisk command, tinged with anger at this new stranger, snapped Benny into action. "Pleased to meet you, sir." He picked up the luggage and beckoned, "Just follow me."

Matt thanked Ted with a handshake, reached for his tackle box and rods, then suddenly turned and gave his full attention to Amy.

"Maybe you'll let me in on some of your secret techniques." A slow, teasing smile provoked her response.

"Maybe?" Her reply was curt and intended to leave him in doubt. *I wouldn't hold my breath if I were you.*

"Just tell me when, o.k.?" With a wink, he turned and started after Benny.

"Hmm, one of those types, eh? Gotta have the last word," muttered Amy as her gaze followed their newest guest. He might resemble Eric, but something was different about this guy.

Expecting him to amble past her and catch up with Benny, Amy noticed his stride was uneven and he walked with a limp. She wondered why. An accident? Birth defect? Disease? Whatever the reason, Matt met the challenge of walking on rough, unfamiliar territory with the confidence of any able-bodied person.

This aura of self-assurance, she noted, was accentuated by the stylish sports clothes, expensive fishing gear, and teasing, sexist remarks. Yet, Amy knew from her studies in psychology, that sometimes such behavior was no more than a mask to hide one's vulnerabilities. Did this guest have a hidden secret? He was a long way from home and why did he choose Pine Lake Lodge?

Chapter Two

Monday morning sunshine peeked through the branches of the birch tree next to Amy's bedroom window beckoning her to get up. But it was the smell of freshly perked coffee and sizzling bacon that drew her out from under the down-filled comforter. Thelma knew how to get folks out of bed without a spoken word.

This high-spirited woman of fifty-eight, whose buxom figure rippled and shook with hearty laughter, embraced each day and wrung every ounce of life out of it. Thelma wasn't hired help in Amy's eyes. She was family and for the past two years, she'd been Amy's Rock of Gibraltar.

The ad Henry placed in the newspaper after his wife, Emily's nervous collapse, requested an experienced cook. Thelma turned out to be much more. Without her housekeeping skills, Amy would have had to drop out of university to help her father. Each time her mother tried to come back and pick up the reins of responsibility, she faced the same problems and ended up back at square one--a nervous wreck!

"Good morning," Amy said as she appeared at the kitchen door. "Coffee smells great."

"You'll be lucky if you get half a cup. Your father drank three before taking off to catch the day's bait. He tells me we have a new guest."

"Sure do. He's in cabin eight." Amy reached for a cup and drained the last of the pot.

"That's all? You must be slipping, girl. I used to get a description of every male who stepped foot on this place."

"Thelma Berton, I never--!" Amy hesitated then began to giggle as she recognized the truth. "Well, I can recall a couple of times."

Thelma was not giving up. "So, how old is he? Single? Good looking?"

"Late twenties, maybe thirty. As far as his marital status is concerned, I have no idea. It's none of my business. And I guess some girls might find him attractive. Subject is closed."

With that, Amy was out the back door leaving Thelma chuckling to herself. She kneaded the bread dough that when baked crispy brown, never failed to melt in their mouths.

Routine activities took up the better part of Amy's day. Thelma did the cooking, so laundry, house cleaning and the general upkeep of nine cottages was left to her. She didn't mind the physical labor. It helped keep her trim and was a pleasant change from the recent mental strain of studying for her degree. After six years, college graduation had come at last.

Laundry was first on her agenda. The smell of freshly washed clothes dancing in the wind mingled with the aroma of wildflowers growing haphazardly beside the clothesline. The last sheet was almost hung when Amy heard an old familiar sound. It was her father, whistling the way he used to whistle as he went from chore to chore.

Lately, though, silent worry replaced his cheery tunes.

"Hi, Daddy. You sound in a good mood. Must have been easy catching minnows this morning?"

"Like giving candy to a baby. There's nothing like Thelma's bread crust to lure them into the net. By the way, I had company ride with me this morning."

"Oh, who?"

"Matt Monroe. I just finished equipping his boat. Told him to try his luck near the rock this end of the island."

Amy's brow wrinkled.

"Think he can manage himself physically around here? I noticed how he walked."

"Seemed to handle getting in and out of the boat just fine. Looks like the independent kind to me."

Amy changed the subject.

"Daddy, have you talked to Jamie lately? I was wondering if business had picked up for him?"

Henry shook his head and replied, "I still can't believe my brother's gone, Amy. Always thought his heart was as strong as an ox. Now the burden of the business is on Jamie's shoulders and he tells me only two of his cottages are rented this week. Sure isn't like it used to be. Come July, you couldn't find a vacancy anywhere in this area. Things are bad all over, honey. That 'For Sale' sign may be the only answer to our worries."

The look of defeat on Henry's face told Amy that he didn't care to sell a part of his life he'd created with his own hands. But, there were still boats to paint, docks to repair, and fish to clean. The work continued. Down time was limited at the lodge. No sooner was one chore completed, than another demanded attention. The constant activity made the hours slip by and before long the sun was falling into the west, signaling the end of another day's accomplishments.

After a day of labor, it was rewarding to relax around

the Lawrence supper table. The blessing Henry gave was short but meaningful. Nostrils inhaled the smell of steaming fresh vegetables and tender meat, oozing with succulent juices. The click of forks clanging against plates as they filled hungry stomachs produced a melody. Crusty bread and rich desserts disappeared when Thelma announced, "Seconds, anyone?"

Casual conversation flowed easily and laughter erupted when Amy repeated a joke she'd heard on the radio.

This banter suddenly turned to silence as Benny announced, "Guess what I found out today?"

"What did you find out, Benny?" asked Thelma.

"Matt, I mean Mr. Monroe, fought in Iraq and was shot down in a helicopter." All eyes focused on the boy. "That's why he limps. He caught the shrapnel from a land mine a guy behind him stepped on. Says he's fortunate that all he got was a bum leg and foot. The other guy was killed."

Amy gasped then grimaced.

"Benny, have you been asking personal questions?"

"No, I was just hauling in some wood for him and I noticed a jacket hanging on the chair. It had a special emblem on it, so I asked what it meant, that's all."

"Well, what did it mean?" asked Henry.

"It was his company's insignia. It had a picture of a medical evacuation helicopter on it. It looked really cool!"

"Sounds as if that man has been through a lot." Henry continued, "He asked for peace and quiet when he arrived. Get my point, Benny?"

"I understand. No pestering."

With the dishes washed, dried, and stacked in rows, Amy had the rest of the evening to herself. After a busy day, she elected to sit on the porch and relax. Some females her age sought the clubs with bright flashing lights and blaring music for their entertainment, but not her. She preferred to watch nature put on its own show. A full moon illuminated a watery stage with strobes of silver. Fireflies flickered and danced in the darkness to the chorus of chanting bullfrogs. Occasionally, the cry of a whip-poor-will joined in.

Amy sighed, closed her eyes and let her thoughts drift. The soft light in cabin eight caught her attention. Her gaze barely made out the silhouette of a man sitting alone—a man who almost met death half way around the world. What had he done before that? Why did he choose Canada? Amy chided herself for her mild curiosity about a summer guest who no doubt would leave as unexpectedly as he'd come. Besides, the ghost of Eric's face still lingered in the background.

Chapter Three

Every three days, it was customary to distribute fresh linen to the occupied cottages at the lodge. Since Matt arrived on Sunday afternoon, and it was now Wednesday, Amy gathered up the necessary sheets and started toward cabin eight. Her auburn curls bounced as she walked and just a hint of blush heightened her natural tanned complexion. Denim shorts and a white peasant blouse fit perfectly on her size eight, five-foot four frame.

She didn't expect to find Matt at the cottage as she was sure he'd be somewhere out on the lake. However, there he was, sitting on the porch with one leg outstretched, the other dangling over the side, and his back propped against the wall. A fishing rod lay beside him amid yards and yards of tangled line. Patiently, his fingers moved back and forth, drawing line in one loop-hole and out the other, trying to unscramble a fisherman's nightmare.

Amy's first reaction was to turn around and go back; but, Matt looked up and saw her. Too late.

"Excuse me," she said. "Do you mind if I change your bed linen?"

"Go right ahead," his eyes remained fixed on the pile of line in front of him. I haven't made it since I've been here."

"Well, that's your choice. I won't be long."

Without comment, Matt continued to study the frustrating, black maze.

Sensing his coolness, Amy went about her task without hesitation. The blankets hung to the floor on one side, and the sheets lay in a wrinkled heap, barely covering the mattress. Obviously, coping with this household chore wasn't high on his list of priorities.

As Amy transformed the bed into a resting place of blue linen and soft, navy blankets, she noticed Matt's periodic glances through the screen door. She quickly gathered the soiled sheets in her arms and was halfway out when he asked, "Do you have a minute? I could use a little help with this line. If you'll hold this end, I'll try to weave my end in and around the holes, and hopefully we'll end up with one straight line."

Matt had a definite problem. There was no way Amy could refuse her help.

"Sure. I've untangled my share of backlashes, believe me."

The sheets landed in an empty lounge chair as she kneeled down to examine the line.

"So, you're an expert in this area, too." He raised his eyebrow and his mordant tone continued. "Sounds like you're a pretty independent gal. Never thought I'd find a feminist way up here in the north woods."

He struck a nerve! She'd been down this road with Eric and his chauvinistic arrogance. Enough was enough!

"You have something against women who can look out for themselves? On second thought, I've got ironing to do." Amy threw down the tangled line and jumped to her feet.

Matt held out a hand to stop her. "Wait, I really do need your help. If you go now, I'll end up spending the rest of my vacation sitting on the porch, slowly going insane with this tangled web. Now you wouldn't want that on your conscience, would you?"

Amy hesitated, then swayed by the pleading in his voice, she joined him as they followed the black line through the maze until the puzzle was solved.

"Thanks," said Matt, "You've proved once again that a man can't do without a woman."

Amy was quick to respond. "Just consider it an extra service." She tempered her words with a brief smile. "We'll add it to your bill."

"Fair enough."

Amy picked up the linens and walked toward the lodge. She puzzled over her encounter with their guest. There was no denying a hint of arrogance in his attitude; but why did he feel it necessary to badger her? Was he hiding behind some carefully constructed façade, or was his true personality showing through?

Not my problem, she decided. *I'm here to change his sheets. In no time, he'll be history.*

Thelma was standing at the sink at the kitchen window with a large wooden spoon in one hand and a bowl full of batter in the other. The smirk on her rosy lips warned Amy that a comment was forthcoming.

Thelma delivered it. "Well, now, you're certainly losing your touch,"

"What do you mean?" Amy crossed the kitchen and threw the sheets into a pile on the laundry room floor.

"Since when does it take almost an hour to change one bed?"

"I was ... busy with Matt," she stammered, "I mean ... he had his fishing line in an awful mess and I was helping him straighten it out."

"Yes, I'm listening. Go on," urged Thelma.

15

"Thelma, you have that twinkle in your eye which means you don't believe a word I'm saying. It's true. I was simply lending a helping hand."

"Amy, I'm real proud of you. You know the Good Book tells us to help one another." Thelma chuckled as the batter she was beating bubbled and spattered over the edge of the bowl. "Especially," she added with a smile, "handsome young strangers."

Exasperated, Amy sighed, "Beat your cake. I'm changing into my suit and taking a swim."

* * *

With the temperature climbing into the high eighties and only an occasional wisp of a breeze giving relief from the heat, Amy dropped her towel on the dock, arched her curvaceous body and dove like a well-trained athlete into the lake. Reaching the bottom in a matter of seconds, she held her breath until she felt her lungs ache. In no hurry to return to the surface, she floated upward and slowly exhaled the air inside of her. The still water shattered as her glistening face appeared. Amy opened her eyes, and directly over-head, against a clear blue sky, was an airplane with a very peculiar, long, stinger-like tail. The airplane kept circling a specific area of the forest at a much lower altitude than she was used to seeing.

Amy decided the Department of Lands and Forest Management must have bought a new aircraft for fighting fires and this was a practice maneuver.

Satisfied with her own explanation of the incident, she swam twenty yards out into the deeper water, changed her direction, and headed back to the dock. She'd have an hour of sun-bathing before Thelma's booming voice announced, "Supper's ready." Those words always drew Benny, Henry and her to the kitchen like a magnet.

For now, the warmth of the sun lulled her into a half-conscience slumber with only the sound of an aircraft still humming in the distance preventing her from falling asleep.

Later that evening, Amy sat down to write her mother a letter. It wasn't an easy task to skirt around the doctor's specific instructions to spare her mom distressing news. She weighed and chose her words carefully to avoid mentioning the fact only three cottages were occupied, the bills were stacking higher each day, and soon the black numbers on the books would turn red. Last week, the bank had required Henry to put the lodge up as collateral in order to secure the loan he needed to pay her mom's bills.

Instead, Amy told her everyone was fine, the weather was beautiful, and the fishing was good. She stopped writing and pondered. Should she tell her mother about their newest guest? After all, what was there to tell, other than he was rather handsome, arrogant, and hated to make beds. Putting her pen to paper, she wrote that they had rented another cottage this week.

After inquiring if there was anything she needed, Amy signed the letter with love and tucked it into an envelope. Lately, though, unanswered questions continued to nag her. Why could her mother not cope? What was the root cause of her collapse? Was she not happy with her life? Had the pressure of the declining tourist trade taken its toll? Amy recalled the times her mom told her of going off to the city while she was barely out of her teens and working as a maid for a wealthy family. Her mom reveled in the sights, shopping, and many activities not available in the country. She even had a boyfriend. That was until Henry convinced her to return home and start Pine Lake Lodge. Did she resent the many years of shared labor? Did she long for her former life? Or was it their present circumstances?

Amy remembered her mother as a lively woman who worked hard alongside her husband and made sure her daughter learned the necessary skills to run a household. They did, however, disagree on one issue—Eric. Her mother saw a shallowness in his character that blinded Amy and on more than one occasion they argued about

17

him.

"Mom, give him a break. He's just overwhelmed with pressure and work. You know he's taking the bar exam soon. Once we're married, you'll see a better side of him."

"I don't like the way he talks to you. He's demanding. Like a spoiled child. Why, he hardly spoke to your father or me the last time he came home with you. I get the feeling we're not good enough. I think you can do better, honey. Use your father as a measuring stick; he's the best."

In the end, Amy realized she was right.

"Oh, well," she sighed, "that's one concern she won't have."

Switching off the light, she silently prayed that her mother could find peace in her life.

Chapter Four

The ringing of the phone interrupted the swishing sound of hot, sudsy water oozing out of Amy's mop as she cleaned the front porch. Her first impulse was to drop everything and rush inside to answer it, but decided instead that Thelma was in the kitchen and could reach it sooner than she. In seconds, Amy barely heard Thelma's side of the conversation over the swishing rhythm of the mop.

Half the porch was finished when Thelma came to the door. "Amy, do you see Henry around? That Williams man from Lakeside Lodge wants to talk to him. And to anyone else who'll listen. I thought he'd never get to the point, and here I am with pies in the oven."

"Tend to your pies, Thelma. I'll go find Daddy. I remember him saying something to Benny at breakfast about putting new planking on the dock in front of cabin one."

The echoing sound of spikes being hammered into the planking resounded in Amy's ears before she reached the

19

dock. It wasn't a day suited to industrious work, as evidenced by the rivulets of sweat that ran down Henry's face. A shimmer of perspiration glistened on Benny's tanned bare back, but the two appeared to ignore the scorching temperature and proceeded vigorously.

"Sorry to interrupt all this activity," Amy joked, "but you're wanted on the phone, Daddy."

Henry uttered a couple of words under his breath, put down his hammer and said, "Take a fiver, Benny. I hope this won't take too long. Who is it, Amy?"

"Stan Williams from down the lake."

Henry looked at her in dismay. "Not long-winded Stan. The last time he called, I was on the phone for an hour."

"That'd suit me fine," said Benny grinning broadly.

"You're not going soft on me now, are you, Benny?" teased Henry as he went for the phone.

Deciding the rest of the scrubbing could wait awhile longer, Amy rolled the legs of her jeans to her knees, sat on a finished portion of the dock, and dangled her legs in the water, in the way she had done as a child. Only then, she liked to kick the surface of the water until it turned white with foamy bubbles. A passing motorboat interrupted her memories. Benny recognized the driver first.

"There goes Mr. Monroe again. He sure likes to fish, doesn't he?"

"How would I know?"

"Oh, I thought you two were getting to know each other. I saw you helping him with his tangled line yesterday."

"I happened to be there at the time, Benny. Any one of us could have done the same thing."

"Well, he asked me this morning if I could show him some of the good spots to try his luck and I told him I had this job to do, but you might be available to show him around."

Amy's mouth flew open and she turned to face Benny

so suddenly she lost her balance and fell into the lake. She came up sputtering and spewing.

"You did what! Since when do you volunteer my time, young man? And what makes you think I'd want to show him around?"

Benny's eyed twinkled and he looked at her in a devilish sort of way.

"Got a rise out of you, didn't I?"

"Wait until I tell Thelma you were teasing me," Amy threatened. "There'll be no seconds on the apple pie tonight."

"Did you say apple pie?" Benny's expression changed at once as he pleaded, "I'm sorry, Amy. I take it all back."

Amy nodded, "You'd better."

"You know I wouldn't do anything like that to you," continued Benny. "But, I did tell Matt to try his luck down there by the shoal."

"I hope you warned him about all the deadheads under the water, Benny. They can mess up a prop pretty badly you know."

"He said he'd watch out for them. Say maybe you should've gone with him to navigate."

"Get out of here," she teased splashing water at the laughing teen and pulled up onto the dock shaking herself off like a wet puppy.

Benny was in retreat when Henry appeared. "What's on your agenda this afternoon, Amy?"

"You mean after I dry off and change clothes? Nothing much. I was scrubbing the porch when Stan called."

"Well, I just volunteered your services. Stan has a group of Boys Scouts camping at his place this week and he needs a five-horsepower motor. Since we aren't using ours, I told him you'd take it down later."

"No problem. I'd enjoy the ride."

"Amy," Benny asked giving her his best wink, "How come your father gets away with volunteering your time and I can't?"

"Gets away with what?" asked Henry.

"Just a little inside joke, Daddy. I'll be ready to go in an hour."

Lakeside Lodge was located at the extreme end of Pine Lake. She basked in the warmth of the four-o'clock sun, even though a stiff wind swept across the lake, sending her small boat crashing into a parade of continuous whitecaps. Seagulls flew against an azure sky, periodically diving for a late afternoon snack.

The channel into Lakeside Lodge was narrower than the main body of the lake, and much calmer water surrounded the area. Amy was careful to cut back on the power, anticipating the occasional menacing log or rock hidden in the shallow water.

Little bodies, some in swim suits, others in the familiar Boy Scout uniform, swarmed all over the grounds of the lodge. Stan was easy to spot. Only a fringe of white hair grew around his bald head. He sent the boys scattering in all directions to make way for Amy's boat to dock. She was greeted like a lost friend, with smiles, handshakes, and squealing voices of delight. Stan explained that for some of the boys boating was a new experience and now with another outboard at their disposal, it would add much to their adventure. In fact, Stan was so appreciative he insisted Amy stay for supper. She protested, but in vain, as Stan's wife called Thelma to say that Amy was dining out this evening. Knowing her host's gift for gab, Amy was sure it would be some time before she returned to Pine Lake Lodge.

Dusk had fallen and darkness was silently closing in when Amy untied her boat and shoved off into the shadows. It was an entirely different feeling on the return trip. A new moon hung low in the heavens, and one by one, stars made their entrance onto the gigantic stage. A whisper of wind gently stirred the surface of the lake.

Traveling at half throttle, enjoying the evening, Amy noticed a large mass about fifty feet from the boat. In the scant moonlight, she made out the outline of what looked like another smaller craft. The thought crossed her mind that perhaps the strong wind earlier in the afternoon had loosened its rope and set it adrift. This had happened occasionally and her father had to tow it back to the dock.

Amy decided to investigate, and if this was the case, she'd save him a trip and bring the boat back herself. Turning her hand-held searchlight to the left, she was startled to find not only a boat, but also a man in it. Immediately, she backed down the motor's throttle, then shut it off.

"Do you need help?" she called.

The response came from a familiar voice.

"Now that's an understatement if I ever heard one."

"Matt! What are you doing out here in the dark? Are you fishing?"

"Does it look like I'm fishing? These are oars in my hands. They're used to row boats."

"Why are you rowing? What's wrong with your motor?"

"I hit one of those deadheads Benny warned me about and knocked off the propeller. Of course, with your experience around boats, you'd know all about that, wouldn't you?"

"You're right." Indignation flared. "I know enough to stay out of water I've been told is hazardous."

"Point taken. Now are you going to tow me back to the lodge or are you planning on letting me row the rest of the way?"

Amy was tempted to tell him he'd mastered the skill so well this far that he'd have no trouble continuing, but on second thought, she held her tongue deciding Matt was obviously tired, angered, and humiliated at finding himself in such a situation. Then too, he was a guest, and they

23

needed the money. Together, they shifted the boats around until they secured the bow line from Matt's boat to the stern of Amy's.

They made slow progress through the blackness. Matt handled the light while Amy concentrated on following its pathway. With narrowed eyes, she scanned the water ahead. Amy fought off the fatigue of the long day and was determined to show Matt she could manage. For some unknown reason, his attitude implied that women were weak. This female determined to prove him wrong as she navigated the boat in the treacherous darkness, but it wasn't until she spied the lights from the lodge illuminating the main dock that she gave a sigh of relief.

Henry was waiting for them with his own searchlight in hand.

"I was getting a little concerned about you two."

"My fault, Henry. I got too engrossed in my fishing and wasn't paying attention to the hidden logs on the shoal. I'm embarrassed to tell you but I wiped out one of your props. Amy spotted me rowing back."

"The prop can be replaced easily enough, Matt. I'm sorry you were inconvenienced, though." He turned his attention to Amy. "Lucky I sent you to Stan's. Matt might still be out there."

Without comment, she turned to Matt with a tongue-in-cheek smile.

Henry went ahead and checked out the disabled motor. Not wishing to linger, Amy made sure her boat was safely secured, picked up her light, and walked toward the lodge.

She was almost off the dock when Matt called to her, "Amy, I guess I'm in your debt. That's the second time this week I've needed your help."

"You're right, Matt. Better stay out of trouble. That bill I mentioned keeps getting longer and longer. Goodnight."

Chapter Five

Amy awakened early Friday morning. She threw on a college sweatshirt and a pair of jeans, splashed some water on her face, ran a brush through tangled curls, and tiptoed down the stairs to the back door. The morning coolness sent little shivers up and down her warm body. Without haste, she started her trek around the shoreline to the boathouse. Tiny frogs jumped helter-skelter with each invading step she took until she reached the ramp. Amy sat with her arms wrapped around her drawn-up knees and watched the birth of a new day.

Morning mist caressed the placid lake, dissipating as the sun's rays brightened the eastern horizon. Robins chirped as they hopped to and fro searching for their first meal of the day in the dew-covered grass, and a rock bass broke the surface of the water to swallow a water bug. Amy tried to center her thoughts on the simple acts of nature she'd just witnessed but the turmoil in her heart outweighed the surrounding serenity. Would this be her last summer at the lodge? The question haunted her daily.

A lone figure stepped onto the main dock, carrying a minnow net and a basket of bread. Amy knew that meant it was seven o'clock and Henry, in his usual routine, was off to catch the day's bait. No matter how few guests were renting cottages, there were always minnows in the bait box. Amy felt that her father needed this time alone to sort out his thoughts and plan for the future. She watched his boat travel down the lake until it was out of sight, then reluctantly, left her sanctuary and returned to the lodge.

"Thank heavens you're up!" Thelma was in a tizzy. "Throw that toast in the trash before everyone in camp forms a bucket brigade."

"What's the problem, Thelma?" Amy smiled as she deposited four pieces of charred bread in the trash. "Not like you to lose it."

"The problem, my dear, is that when your father gets back from catching minnows, he's taking the folks in cabin two out on the lake for the day and I'm packing a picnic lunch. Now—this instant." The pile of buttered bread grew higher and higher. "You're on your own as far as breakfast is concerned."

"Well, thank the good Lord all our problems aren't this serious," Amy mocked. "A fifty percent drop in business pales in comparison."

"I know you're worried about the future of this place, Amy."

"Shouldn't I be?"

"Amy," Thelma stopped buttering bread and looked intently at her, "you're twenty-four-years old—-too young to carry such a heavy burden."

"I'm part of this family, Thelma."

"But no one expects you to shoulder the success or failure of this lodge. It's been rough enough on you getting over that jerk, Eric. I would love to see you happily married."

"Thelma, marriage wouldn't solve anything. I just can't walk away from Daddy, especially, with Mom in the condition she's in. Besides, who on earth would I marry around here?"

"Would you settle for Ted down at the marina?"

"Just to set the record straight once and for all, Ted and I are best of friends. Nothing more. Subject is closed."

The sound of Benny coming down the stairs for breakfast provided a timely interruption.

"Henry left instructions that you're to paint the outside window trim on all the windows around cabin three, Benny," Thelma said as this hungry teenager settled down at the table. "The paint, brush, and ladder are all waiting for you in the storage shed."

"Sounds like you've got a full day ahead of you, young man," Amy remarked. "I believe that calls for an extra egg or two." Three eggs sizzled as they hit the spitting bacon fat.

"Suits me fine," Benny grinned. "I need all the energy I can get. It's hard work climbing to the top of that ladder."

"Well, soon as you've finished eating, take this basket over to cabin two before you start painting," Thelma said. "Henry will be ready to go in about thirty minutes. You know it takes him a short while to get the bait."

* * *

By lunch, Amy finished ironing the last shirt in the laundry basket, Thelma's freshly baked bread was sitting on the cupboard, and Benny reported that half the windows were painted. He felt sure a couple of hours should finish the job.

After clearing away the lunch dishes, Amy mentally checked off another chore on her list and moved on to cleaning the dusty, smudged bay window in front of the lodge. Just as she dipped her cleaning cloth into the bucket of water, a startling cry shattered the stillness.

Amy jumped off the chair and ran down the steps.

Before she reached the bottom, she heard another cry for help. There was no doubt in her mind that the cries came from cabin three. It had to be Benny. A rush of adrenalin raced through her and she breathlessly reached the cabin to observe white paint splashed in all directions, a fallen ladder, and Benny lying on the ground. His normally healthy glow gave way to a strained ashen mask. His lips were white and his right forearm, bent at an awkward angle, was obviously broken.

"Amy, it's my arm," Benny gasped from the pain and his breath came in short, fast, shallow pants, "I fell off the ladder. A rung must have broken."

Amy glanced at the fallen ladder beside them. Sure enough, the fifth rung from the top was split into two jagged pieces.

"Don't move your arm," she commanded.

Thelma came running up to them, wheezing and shaken by the scene before her.

"Benny, what happened? I heard you yell, and Amy took off like a bolt of lightning."

"The ladder broke and he fell on his arm. Of all days for Daddy to be out on the lake!" Suddenly, Amy remembered Benny told them the insignia on Matt's jacket was a medical evacuation helicopter. "Thelma, make him comfortable, but don't move his arm. I'm going for Matt.

She took off toward Matt's cabin before there was time to ask questions."

Chapter Six

As Amy drew closer to cabin eight, her breath became shorter and perspiration streamed down her forehead. Once, she almost tripped over a wandering tree root. Finally, reaching her destination, she ran up the steps and pounded on the door. No response. Silence.

"Oh, no, he can't be away," she cried aloud. "Matt? Matt? Are you in there?"

Matt called from the shoreline, "I'm down here. What's all the fuss?"

Amy jumped off the porch and ran to him, her composure deteriorating, "It's Benny! He needs help! He fell off the ladder."

This time there was no bantering. Just questions.

"Is he conscious? Is he bleeding? What was he doing?"

The answers came quickly from Amy's parched lips as they made their retreat. She squelched the urge to break into a run but kept pace with Matt who bore his handicap with steadfast determination. Finally, they reached the

29

injured boy's side and Matt examined Benny's arm.

"He needs to see a doctor. The arm is fractured. The first thing to do is put it in splints." Matt took a quick look around and his eyes focused on the woodpile. "Amy, hand me that short slab of wood—-the one about twelve inches long. And I need rope or strips of cloth, anything to tie his arm down."

There was no doubt. Matt was in command of the situation. After handing Matt the slab, Amy took off running toward the lodge in search of material, while Thelma, using her apron, mopped beads of sweat that popped out on Benny's face. As Amy approached the porch, she saw the discarded towel she'd planned to use to clean the window draped across the arm of the chair. She grabbed it and raced back to see that Matt had Benny's arm resting on the makeshift splint.

"Just what we need," Matt said as he began to tear the towel into strips. "Benny, I'll try to do this as gently as possible, but you're going to feel some pain. I have to tie your arm to the board. It keeps it from moving but you're going to be fine."

Benny nodded his head, moaning and biting his lip as Matt secured each strip of material to the board.

It was obvious to Amy that the materials Matt used for a splint were makeshift, but the skill with which he used them were nothing less than professional.

"I'll go get my keys and bring the boat to the dock," said Amy, as once again she dashed off to the lodge, grabbed her purse, and ran to the boat. Untying the rope, she jumped on the deck, hopped over the seats, and pulled the starting cord. The sudden roar of the motor was a joyful sound. She threw the shift lever forward and maneuvered the craft toward cabin three.

Immediately, Thelma and Matt appeared, half carrying Benny who looked ready to faint. Amy held the boat close to the dock while Matt stepped inside and reached for the boy. Thelma waited until Matt had a good grip him and then stepped back.

Amy yelled above the motor noise, "Tell Daddy not to worry. I'll call when we're ready to start back."

Matt arranged Benny's arm as comfortable as possible, then sat down on the seat next to him. With a wave to Thelma, Amy turned toward Ted's marina.

A strong wind aroused the lake. Waves tumbled over waves, each growing higher, until finally, a spray of water leaped over the gunnel and trickled down inside. The impact of the fast moving boat hitting the choppy water produced a series of bumps and bounces. Amy saw the pain in Benny's face each time the boat hit a new wave. Fortunately, his torment was over in less than thirty minutes. Once at the marina, Bob, Ted's brother, helped Matt get Benny into Amy's car while she secured the boat. It wouldn't take long now before Dr. Willis would take over.

Once at the clinic, Amy ran in to seek the receptionist assistance.

"Nancy, Benny broke his arm. He needs to see the doctor right now."

"Grab that wheelchair by the door and we'll get him right in."

In less than five minutes, Dr. Willis was in the examining room.

"Hello there, young man. I see Amy has brought me a patient."

As Matt helped Benny out of the wheelchair and onto the examining table, Amy introduced him to the town's only doctor. The two men shook hands and Amy proceeded to give the details of the accident.

"This is one of the best emergency first-aid jobs I've seen in a long time," remarked Dr. Willis, examining Benny's arm. "I've known you most of your life, Amy, but I never knew you to excel in the medical field."

"Oh, the credit doesn't belong to me!" gasped Amy. "Matt's responsible, believe me."

Dr. Willis raised his bushy eyebrows in a questioning manner. "Do you work in the medical profession?"

"No sir, I was trained in the U.S. Army to work with a Med-Evac team in Iraq."

"Well, son," Dr. Willis looked at Matt with admiration coupled with sympathy, "You've seen a lot worse than this then, haven't you?"

"Yes, sir. Much worse."

Sensing she was no longer needed, Amy excused herself and called Benny's parents to notify them of the accident.

His mom, anxious to see her son, told Amy she'd meet her immediately. For the past two hours, Amy'd been running on adrenalin and suddenly she felt exhausted. Her legs went limp and she let her body ease down onto the comfortable leather cushions. Her eyes closed and she felt as though she could sleep the rest of the day. Her reprieve, however, was short-lived. Benny's mother arrived just as Matt and Dr. Willis entered the waiting room.

Addressing both women, Dr. Willis explained that x-rays showed the injury was a simple fracture.

"I gave him an anesthetic. As soon as it takes effect," continued Dr. Willis, "I'll set and cast his arm. He should be out of here in an hour."

It was agreed that Benny should stay at his parent's home for the time being. There was no point in returning to the lodge with an injury. Amy would just have to add the extra chores to her workload. The summer's burden continued to grow.

Chapter Seven

Amy and Matt were half a mile down the road on their return trip when Amy remembered that Thelma was waiting for her call. The post office had a pay phone, so she decided to stop there. Besides, no one had picked up the mail in a couple of days. Matt sat in the car while she dashed into the building and made the call. Her conversation was brief; Benny was staying in town but she and Matt would be home soon.

Back in the car, Amy quickly scanned the day's mail before starting the engine. In the pile was a white business envelope with the return address sporting a logo and large black letters. At first glance, she recognized the Civic Hospital stationery. Another bill. Her hazel-green eyes clouded and she heaved a sigh.

Matt observed her change in demeanor "You okay? Something in your mail upset you?"

"I'm sorry, I didn't realize it showed."

Matt placed his hand on her shoulder and gave her a

gentle squeeze. "It may surprise you, Amy, but I'm a good listener."

His unexpected touch set her nerves tingling and she stumbled over her response, "I ... uh ... I don't want to bore you with problems. You requested peace, remember."

"Why don't you let me be the judge of that?" The insistence in his eyes and the plea in his voice broke her reserve.

"You asked for it." Amy smiled weakly. "Yes, I'm upset! This is another hospital bill."

"Hospital bill?"

"Mom's. She's been in a psychiatric ward off and on for the past two years."

"I'm sorry."

"Me, too. The pressures and demands of life at the lodge became too much for her. She can't handle responsibilities."

"That's why you work so hard here?"

"One of them." Amy took a deep breath to regain her composure before she continued. "It's not just Mom being in the hospital. Daddy's practically broke. His financial resources have about run out. Insurance helps with the hospital. Some. But we've got all these bills for the resort, too."

"That explains the 'For Sale' sign down by the shoreline."

"Yes, last week Daddy decided it was the only sensible thing to do. I don't know which of us hurt the most when we pounded that sign into the ground. He's been here thirty-five years."

"That's a long time. Be hard to give it up."

"The sky-rocketing cost of gas and oil has stopped most folks from traveling. It's got us over a barrel and that goes for every other resort in the area."

"From what I've seen today, you seem to be able to handle the unexpected pretty decently." Matt's steady gaze unnerved her and she squeezed the steering wheel to keep her hand from trembling.

"Thanks for the vote of confidence. Time will tell. Appreciate the shoulder, too. It helps to unload."

"Anytime."

He smiled that smile again. This time the warm tingles spread from head to toe. She was relieved when she saw the lake ahead. She parked the car in its usual spot and she and Matt headed to the boat. They sat down and Amy had her hand on the starter cord when Ted came running down the ramp, yelling, "Bob tells me Benny fell off the ladder. How is he?"

"Dr. Willis says it's a simple fracture. He'll have his arm in a cast for a few weeks," explained Amy.

"You be careful down there, girl. You folks don't need anymore headaches."

"Don't worry, Ted. See you." Amy waved goodbye and once again put her hand to the starter.

The motor had not yet fired when Matt commented, "Sounds to me like someone is worried about you."

Amy lightly brushed aside his insinuating remark.

"Oh, Ted has always been like a big brother to me. He knows I can take care of myself."

"Be careful now," teased Matt, "you wouldn't want to become too independent. Hurts a man's ego, you know."

For a moment Amy's body stiffened. They'd crossed fire on this subject once before.

"Hey, I ... "

Matt stopped her before she could reply. "Just kidding. Start the engine, Captain."

Amy gave him a long, hard look then ignited the motor and in moments, they were on their way to Pine Lake Lodge. The whitecaps seen earlier in the afternoon were mere ripples now. The water offered no resistance and the boat skimmed its surface leaving a foamy wake behind. A late afternoon sun sank into the western sky, leaving a bank of clouds laced with purple and gold. Around the shoreline, white birches cast their shadows on the water while an old porcupine ambled onto a log to give passing strangers a defiant stare. Amy's spirits lifted as the cool of the evening refreshed her senses. She looked at Matt sitting on the bow of the boat, deep in his own thoughts. Yes, she'd seen a side of his personality that bordered on arrogance, but today she saw a sensitive side as well.

She wondered what she would have done without him this afternoon. It wasn't simply the first-aid he'd given to Benny. It went deeper. His presence alone had comforted her.

As the lodge came into view, Amy backed off on the throttle. Henry, heard the approaching boat, and was ready to catch the bow.

"Well, now", he said as the boat glided toward the dock, "you two have had quite a day of it, haven't you?"

"I'll second that, Daddy. Matt, thank you for all you did today."

"That goes for me, too," Henry assured him. "I know you came up here for peace and quiet, but we appreciate what you did for Benny."

"I was glad to be of help, Henry."

"Listen, Thelma has supper on the table and she insists you join us. What do you say?"

"Well, if the food's as good as the company, I'd be a fool to say no. Sounds great to me."

The meal was up to Thelma's excellent standard. The roast beef oozed succulent juices; steam rose from golden corn on the cob; creamy whipped potatoes filled a large bowl and two lemon meringue pies sat on the cupboard. Even though Amy felt ravenous, she wasted no time in relating the details of Benny's accident and the doctor's diagnosis to her father and Thelma. Matt was content to concentrate on second helpings. Periodically, he'd offer a comment or two.

The meal was almost over when Henry said, "Well, my day certainly wasn't as exciting as yours, but I did see something that caught my attention."

Everyone turned questioning eyes in his direction.

"What was it, Henry?" Matt asked.

"The strangest looking aircraft I ever did see. For a moment, I thought this might be a UFO, but it stayed around too long."

"Describe it, Daddy."

"It looked like a plane, but there was a long device of some sort attached to the tail."

"I saw that, too," Amy exclaimed. "It kept circling one area over and over. I decided it must belong to the Forest Rangers."

"Not unless it's something new they're using." Henry shook his head. "I've never known them to use planes like that one to fight fires."

"Seems like we have a mystery on our hands," Thelma concluded.

"Oh, someone in town will know and we'll find out soon enough." Henry ended the discussion.

After a few minutes of small talk, Matt thanked Thelma for the meal and excused himself, stating that he intended to get an early start fishing in the morning. Shortly after Matt left, Amy glanced at the clock and decided to turn in, too. Yawning goodnight she went to her room and prepared for bed. She tried to dismiss the day's events, but they kept playing like a DVD over and over in her mind. She saw the pain on Benny's ashen face, she felt the warmth of Matt's fingers on her shoulder, and she heard the humming of a mystery plane.

Chapter Eight

The roar of what sounded like the lawn mower shattered the morning stillness and Amy's eyes shot open. It couldn't be Benny cutting the grass. He was with his parents. The roar changed to a softer putt-putt, then silence.

Curiosity got the better of her. She jumped out of bed and ran to the window. Out on the water, a pontoon aircraft glided on the water toward the dock. Henry stood ready to catch the tip of the wing as it pulled up beside him. A small door opened, and out jumped Larry Rogers, Amy's cousin. Larry made a living flying fishermen to and from the numerous rivers and lakes in the area. Behind him, another man climbed down from the plane.

"Oh, great," Amy thought, "Larry's brought us another guest." She was full of anticipation as she watched Henry shake hands with the two men. However, there was something strange; no one was attempting to unload any luggage or fishing gear.

Dressing quickly, she dashed into the bathroom to

freshen up, then descended the stairs to the kitchen where Thelma sat reading a new cookie recipe. At the sound of Amy's footsteps, she raised her head from the paper and started to tease, "My, my, aren't we the lady of leisure."

"Don't say another word. I know I overslept."

"Can't say I really blame you. Yesterday's excitement took a lot out of me, too. This ole gal ain't what she used to be."

"Fact is I wouldn't be down here yet if it hadn't been for the roar of Larry's plane waking me. He brought a man with him. I wonder who he is?"

"Well, I can't sit around all day waiting to find out." Thelma got up from the table. "These cookies must be baked for the shore dinner this afternoon. Remember?"

Amy had forgotten all about the shore dinner. Once a week, she and Thelma spent most of the morning packing picnic baskets with all the necessary food and utensils for a fish fry out on the shoreline for their guests. Iron skillets, long-handled forks, spatulas, tin cups, and plates were tucked into a large wicker basket. The buttered bread, baked beans, pickles, and desserts were the last to be packed. Amy's work was cut out for her, especially since she had a late start on the preparations this morning.

As she set to work, she noticed that Larry was staying longer than normal. Time spent in the air meant money to him. Something in the back of Amy's mind told her that Larry's passenger was not a fisherman. Taking a glance out the window, she saw three men coming towards the lodge. Larry took up the rear as Henry and the stranger walked together. Every so often, they stopped and Henry pointed to one thing or another. It was obvious to Amy that he was giving a tour of the place.

Foot steps hit the steps of the front porch and the voices of the men grew louder. Henry opened the screen door and the men entered.

"Amy, can you come here?" Henry called from his

office.

Dropping the bundle of forks she was counting, she walked toward her father, anxious to find out what this man wanted.

"Hey, Larry." Her eyes moved to the man dressed in tan pants and matching jacket. Across the front of the jacket, three words stood out in red letters--Canadian Uranium Company.

Questions flashed through Amy's mind. Why was a miner in this area? Why was he interested in Pine Lake Lodge? And why did Henry want her to meet him?

"Tom Evans, this is my daughter, Amy."

"Pleased to meet you, Amy." The stranger extended his hand.

"Tom works for a mining company," Henry explained. "He heard we have a lodge for sale and Larry flew him in to look things over."

"This is quite a lovely place you folks have here."

"Thank you," Amy said, "but I'm a little confused. Are you interested in running a fishing lodge?"

"Not exactly. You see, my company has found a sizable amount of uranium ore a few miles from Pine Lake, and we need a base camp. Rather than build one from scratch, it would save a lot of time if we move right into an establishment such as this one. Everything we need is here—cabins for the men, kitchen, and dining facilities."

"Oh, I see," was all she could stammer. Her stomach knotted and she could feel her cheeks redden with anger.

Tom Evans took no notice of Amy's change in composure. Business was on his mind. "Well, Henry, let's start negotiating."

Amy couldn't bring herself to look at her father. She knew if she looked into his eyes and saw any of the hurt she was feeling at this moment, it would destroy them both. For Henry's sake, she excused herself before she lost control. With her head lowered, she left the office and ran out to the back porch. Tears streamed down her cheeks. Reality hit her like the force of a fighter's first punch. All along Amy knew that the lodge must be sold, but she visualized the resort as it always had been, for fishermen and vacationers. A mining company? Repulsive! Thelma opened the door. "Amy, what's wrong, girl? I've never known your father to upset you like this."

"It wasn't Daddy, Thelma. That man, Tom Evans, wants to turn this place into a base camp for a mining company. Can you believe that?"

"That what your father wants?"

"They're discussing the terms right now. I guess I didn't fully understand how desperate Daddy is to sell."

Placing her arm around Amy's shoulder, Thelma gave her a squeeze. "Your father isn't going to make any rash decisions; so, pull yourself together and let's get the rest of the shore dinner prepared before we both lose our jobs."

Amy half-smiled as she brushed the last tear from her cheek and started toward the waiting door. Thelma could always be counted on to put life into its proper perspective.

Chapter Nine

Amy hadn't crossed paths with her father since morning, and it was now time to pack the boats and journey up the lake. Everyone gathered at the main dock while Henry gave directions. At the last minute, Amy decided to change into jeans. When she returned, the only boat left was Matt's.

"It looks like your only alternative is to swim or ride with me."

"And what would you prefer?" she baited.

"A marathon swim for the guest's enjoyment would round out the day's entertainment, don't you agree?" His easy smile and lingering look demanded a reply.

"Don't tempt me; the challenge might be worth it." Amy yanked on the rope, threw it over the boat's gunnel, and hopped up on the bow. "We might, however, be late for one of Daddy's famous fish fries." She paused before adding, "and I wouldn't want that on my conscience."

Within thirty minutes, the site for the shore dinner was

a hive of activity. Henry was the chef on these outdoor excursions. He loved to fry fish and years of experience taught him well. Thelma gladly handed him the reins, as it gave her a well-deserved break from the kitchen.

Henry split the pine firewood into manageable pieces and placed them inside a circle of rocks. A rectangular grill lay over the spitting, crackling fire, and supported the two large iron skillets. Intense heat sent the oil in the skillets soaring to a perfect temperature for frying fish. Soon, the fillets turned a crispy brown under Henry's skilled watchful eyes.

While the fish fried, the beans bubbled in a pot on a cooler side of the grill. Amy and Thelma unpacked the baskets of home-made bread, potato salad, pickles, condiments and chocolate chip cookies. The aroma of cooking food drifted over the area enticing all to pick up a plate and form a line.

Amy observed from her many outings that eating one's dinner on the shoreline in the invigorating fresh air whets even the smallest appetite, but it didn't work for her this time. Tonight, was different. Tom Evan's words were ringing in her ears, "Everything we need is here ... " made eating out of the question.

While everyone eagerly went back for seconds, Amy slipped away from the laughter and conversation to a quieter place. She sat on a fallen tree that lay outstretched in the mirror-like shallows. Tiny minnows swam up to the surface and nibbled at her fingers as she dipped her hand into the cool water. Robins sang their evening song in the trees overhead as if to ease her troubled mind.

At the sound of crackling branches, Amy turned to see Matt looking down at her.

"Is this a private party, or is anyone welcome? I noticed you slipped away without eating."

"I have to warn you, I'm not very good company."

"Are you still upset about Benny?"

"No. It's something else. I cried on your shoulder yesterday. I don't mean to make a habit…"

"Hey, now listen. My shoulder can handle it. What's the problem?"

"You probably saw a plane land on the lake this morning. It belongs to my cousin, Larry. He flew in with a man who heard we're selling the lodge and he wanted to look it over."

"Well, that's encouraging, isn't it?" Matt lowered himself to the ground and propped his upper body up with one elbow.

"Matt, he represents a uranium mining company and he wants to turn Pine Lake Lodge into a base camp!" A tremor broke her voice. "Can you imagine what will become of it?"

"Mining camps aren't a popular tourist attraction, are they?" His tone softened. "How does your father feel about it?"

"I haven't been able to talk to him yet. We've both been too busy all day. I can't tell him how I feel— especially, if he's made up his mind to sell. It's a hard decision. I can't put doubts in his mind."

Matt ran his hand down his right leg. "Life isn't always easy, is it?"

"No argument from me. First, it was Mom and her problems and now this whole mess. Why do we humans struggle so? Look around you. Nature has it altogether— balanced, serene, beautiful."

"From what I've read, that's how its Maker intended."

"This may sound crazy," Amy confessed, "but from the time I could handle a canoe, I'd paddle around the lake when something upset me and its peacefulness always calmed me down."

"Great idea! Let's do it as soon as we get back?"

"You sure you can paddle a canoe?" Her smile was teasing.

"Are you willing to take the risk?" His tone was playful; his challenge was worth it.

Chapter Ten

A tender glow from an exiting sun fell on the western horizon by the time Matt and Amy pushed off from the beach in their cedar canoe. Golden treetops reflected in the still water. Along the shoreline, a bullfrog sang his throaty baritone love chant. Before long, he was joined by a chorus of sopranos. In the center of the lake, a loon swam in circles calling his mate.

"The loon's call is melancholy." Amy maneuvered her paddle around some lily pads. "Seems like he's upset tonight. Can't find his partner. They mate for life, you know."

"Too bad the human race couldn't take a lesson from Mother Nature." Was that contempt Amy heard in Matt's voice? "Sure hasn't been my experience."

Amy quit paddling, turned, and looked into disillusioned eyes. "I…I'm not sure I understand, Matt."

"I'm speaking from experience. I've been divorced for two years now."

The confession was unexpected. Amy's voice softened. "How long were you married?"

"Four years—we married right out of college. Too young and naïve. The war didn't help either. My National Guard unit was called up and we shipped out for Iraq. The man she married was not the same man that came home. A land mine tore my foot and leg up pretty badly. I was sent home immediately. Christie couldn't handle the surgeries and months of therapy."

They both stopped paddling and the silence spoke for itself.

After another deep breath, Matt continued, "My injury interfered with her life style. We worked hard and we played hard the first three years of our marriage. Then out of the blue, it was over. No more Colorado ski trips, no more scuba diving in the Bahamas, dancing 'til dawn; you get the picture. She didn't sign on to take care of an invalid."

"Invalid? You do fine!"

"Yes, I do, but only after a lot of blood, sweat, and tears. Fourteen months of physical therapy put me on my feet again. I was determined to show everyone that Christie's leaving wouldn't hold me back. It's ironic, but in the long run, she did more for me than if she'd stayed. They tell me time heals all wounds. We'll see."

Matt's words pierced the scab of her own recent wounds. She longed to put Eric's memory behind her. As they drifted over the tranquil surface, the canoe sought its own course.

"Do you miss her?"

Matt paused before answering. "I did for a while. But not anymore. I realize now that our beliefs about life and marriage are different. Maybe the war changed me—made me realize who I am. She couldn't face that reality. She sure wasn't willing to try. It's just who she is. Looking back, I can honestly say that I don't think our marriage would have survived, anyway."

"I … uh, I came close to making a mistake in judgment, too."

"Oh, yeah?"

"My fiancé and I broke up four months ago. Eric was the controlling type. He tried to fit me into a mold that really wasn't me."

"That usually leads to trouble. I'm sorry it didn't work out for you, but you probably did the right thing."

"I keep telling myself I did. I'm not sure. The heart has a way of ruling the head."

As twilight turned into darkness, lights from the lodge beckoned them home. One by one, stars appeared overhead as Amy and Matt paddled in tandem. The silence was comfortable. Amy carefully stepped from the canoe when they reached the beach and held it steady while Matt got out. Together, they pulled the craft out of the water and turned it over. She bent down to pick up the paddles.

"Amy." Matt's voice was low and softer than she'd ever heard it. "This evening was special. It's hard to explain, and I don't expect you to understand, but just know I won't forget it."

He moved toward her and she smelled the scent of his body, warm from the physical paddling, inches from her face. Matt reached out with both hands and gently pulled on her shoulders closing the gap between them. The paddles fell from her grip to the sand as his arms encircled her yielding frame. Resistance was futile. Strong hands molded her putty-like body to his and the tingles she felt exploded into sparks of desire. Breathing was difficult as Matt's searching lips found their mark and his demand deepened. The palm of her hand inched its way up his chest, across his angular jaw and caressed the back of his neck.

Suddenly, the moment was over. Barely touching her flaming cheek with the back of his hand, he withdrew murmuring a husky, "Goodnight." Turning away, he walked into the deepening shadows.

Amy's hands shook, her heart raced, and trembling knees gave out beneath her as she fell to the sand. What was that all about? If she didn't know better, she'd have sworn she'd been dreaming. How dare he lean on her sympathy, awaken feelings that longed to be explored then walk away as though nothing had happened!

It took several minutes for Amy to regain her composure. Sitting there alone, she thought of the men in her life. As a teenager, romances came and went like the seasons, college men found her attractive, especially Eric, but this one was definitely in a class all his own. She may not understand Matt's sudden departure, but one thing she did know for certain. It would be a long time before she put the memory of that kiss behind her.

Chapter Eleven

Henry was on his second cup of coffee when Amy joined him at the table. His wrinkled brow accentuated the troubled look in his eyes, and the muscles in his jaw were drawn and tight. One look and she knew he hadn't slept.

"Get yourself a cup of coffee and come sit. You're not going to like what I have to tell you."

Amy poured herself a cup, sat down across the table from her father, and braced herself for the inevitable.

"That strange looking airplane we've been seeing the past week or so belongs to the mining company. It's built to take special pictures that show where the ore lies. According to Evans, they've located a sizeable amount just four or five miles southwest of here and they'll need a base camp soon. With this frantic search for energy sources, they don't want to take time to build one."

Henry took another sip of coffee and cleared his throat "I'm not happy about selling to a mining company. You know that, but there isn't going to be a reserve to tide us over the winter. When you operate a seasonal business, it can hurt."

"I know you're doing what you feel is best, Daddy. Of course, I'm upset, but I support your decision."

"It helps to hear you say that, honey." Henry drained his cup. "Here we are talking like we have to leave tomorrow, and I haven't even signed any papers. Evans has to return to the head office in Toronto and get their final approval on the deal. He wasn't sure when he'd get back up, but thought the board would meet within the next couple weeks."

"Meanwhile, we have a lodge to run," Amy said.

"And I have a leaky boat to repair." Henry pushed in his chair, walked to the screen door and let it slam in its usual way behind him.

Amy felt better now that she and her father had confronted the situation. It wasn't the best way to start her day, but she accepted his final decision. For now, she comforted herself with the knowledge that the board of directors still had to approve the transaction.

The sale of the lodge wasn't the only thing on her mind this morning. She puzzled over Matt's behavior. The more she thought about the way he had aroused her feelings then casually walked away ignited that 'how dare he' attitude she experienced with Eric. And just when she was beginning to think be had a soft side after all.

One thing she knew: she wasn't ready to face him this morning. The sound of his voice sent her scurrying upstairs to make the beds. After several minutes, Thelma entered the kitchen and called, "Amy, you going to town today? Matt has a letter he needs to have mailed."

"Probably. Daddy's too busy and errands need to be run." She peeked over the banister to be sure Thelma was alone. "Just give me a minute to finish up here and I'll be on my way."

The wind played havoc with Amy's hair as she guided

the small aluminum craft around the lily pads and out into the open water. Normally, she'd have passed a half dozen boats on the trip to the marina, but there wasn't a soul on the lake today. It wasn't a good sign.

Docking her boat at the marina, Amy secured the rope and walked to her car. She was half way to town when she was forced to a stop. Taking up more than its share of the dirt road was a sleek, white Lexus. Inside, sat two women. Amy guessed one to be in her fifties and the other, a young blond, about her own age. Amy got out of her vehicle and walked over to a man who was putting a jack into the trunk. She saw a deflated tire in the gravel road.

"Excuse me, I'm on my way to town. Would you like me to take your tire to the garage?"

"Well, now, young lady, I'd appreciate that. We're looking for a place to stay for awhile. We've been traveling the Trans Canada and decided to take a side trip. I'm tired of swimming pools and motels. Want some natural peace and quiet. Maybe a little fishin', too."

Amy was quick to respond. "You came to the right place. Just happens we have some vacancies at our lodge. You'll have to leave your car at the marina, then travel three miles by boat."

"Sounds great to me. Let me check with my wife."

Moving to the front of the car, he opened the door and said, "How 'bout it, hon? It'd do us good to rest over awhile."

Instantly, the younger woman started, "Get real Father, it's bad enough we had a flat on a deserted road with nothing but a one-horse town behind us! We passed several good-looking motels on the main highway."

"Sonja, this is your father's vacation, too. Now, he's been patient with us, so if he wants to do some fishing, he's entitled. Sounds rather quaint—a lodge accessible only by water. I'm all for it."

"That settles it then. I'm Lyle Newman, and this is my

wife, Elaine, and our daughter, Sonja."

"Hi. I'm Amy Lawrence."

The older woman smiled; the younger nodded, then turned away, sweeping her shoulder-length hair behind ears pierced with diamond studs.

Amy went on to explain, "I have to run a few errands, but I shouldn't be more than an hour. You could wait at the marina. It's just a couple miles down the road."

"We'll be waiting." said Lyle. "Here, let me put this tire in your trunk. I'm already a mess."

Amy got back into her car and managed to squeeze around the Lexus. In a matter of minutes, she came into town and left the flat at Ivan's garage, telling the owner that Mr. Newman would pick it up on his way out.

"Hear your dad may be selling out to that mining company, eh, Amy?"

Annoyed that rumors were flying around already, she shot back, "We aren't packing yet, Ivan. Don't believe all you hear."

Continuing her errands, Amy stopped at the post office to deposit the bundle of mail from the lodge. As she put the letters into the slot, she noticed that Matt's letter was addressed to Dr. Robert Monroe. Amy wondered if this was his father. He hadn't told her anything about his family last night.

After a quick stop at Jake's to pick up a few groceries, Amy headed back to join the waiting Newmans. She arrived at the marina to find a mountain of luggage, two smiling parents, and one disgruntled daughter.

"Do you intend to put all of us and our luggage in this?" Sonja pointed to the aluminum boat with Lawrence painted on the side.

Sonja was right. Her craft would never handle the extra load, so she turned to Lyle and said, "I'll ask Ted over there if he can help us out."

Inside the marina, Ted was busy repairing an outboard

motor. At the sound of Amy's footsteps, he looked up and called, "Hi, beautiful. How are you? I thought that was your car. Those folks in the Lexus been here about forty-five minutes. Know 'em?"

"I'm taking them down to the lodge, but I need your help if you can spare the time. All that luggage is too much for my boat."

"All you have to do is ask. You know that."

Out on the dock, Amy made the introductions. She noticed how quickly Sonja's attitude changed once Ted appeared on the scene. Her smile was radiant as she announced she was riding with him.

Conversation over the motors' noise was difficult, so everyone sat back and enjoyed the scenic ride. From the smiles of contentment on both Lyle and Elaine's faces, Amy could tell they were pleased with their decision. A quick look in Ted's direction showed Sonja stretched out with her long, tanned legs dangling over the boat's gunnel. Every now and then she squealed in delight as a wave sprayed cool water in her direction.

Henry was finishing his repair job as the two boats drew alongside the dock. Amy saw the look of surprise and pleasure on his face when she explained how the Newmans came to be her passengers. He decided cabin seven would accommodate the new guests comfortably. An uneasy feeling stirred in the pit of Amy's stomach as she realized Matt would be next door to the long-legged blond.

"So what!" she scolded herself as she led the way to the cabin and opened its door for their guests. As Elaine awed over the quaintness of the logs and the fieldstone fireplace, Amy noticed that Ted made one trip after another hauling luggage from the boat to the porch. It appeared to her that he was going into minute detail explaining the best fishing spots on the lake to Lyle while Sonja leaned on the railing looking at him as though mesmerized by each word. There was no doubt in Amy's mind Ted would be a frequent visitor this week. Sonja had cast her spell.

Chapter Twelve

The morning sun danced on the sparkling water and wispy clouds passed overhead confirming the radio announcer's forecast, "No rain today, folks. Another perfect day for our summer visitors."

"Few as they may be," whined Amy. Then she remembered the Newmans. That was a lucky break stumbling into them. She'd check later to see if they needed anything. Right now, she had another chore, but she kept putting it off. The linens in cabin eight were due for a change, but Amy wasn't ready to confront Matt. Since the night on the beach, he hadn't made any attempt to explain his behavior and despite her curiosity, Amy wouldn't ask him. She wondered if he was purposely avoiding her, too.

Chores around the kitchen kept her busy until she knew she couldn't put off changing the linen any longer.

Reaching into the cupboard, she piled her arms high with sheets, pillowcases, and towels and started toward Matt's cottage. She needn't have worried about any confrontation, since she could see from a distance he was not alone.

Sitting on the front porch was Sonja. She could have been a model straight out of any of the recent fashion magazines. The make-up was subtle, the revealing halter top and matching shorts were stylish and eye-catching, the leather sandals, no doubt, Italian. To top it off, a golden tan covered her curvaceous body—most of it visible. Amy felt like Cinderella before the ball in her tee-shirt and denims.

Before she reached the steps, Sonja started, "Amy, now you didn't tell me I'd have such an interesting neighbor. Kept that little secret to yourself, eh?" She flashed a flirtatious smile at Matt.

Color flooded his face as he got out of his chair and changed the subject. "Hi! Need some help? You've got an armful."

"No, thank you. I'll manage. I see you two have met."

Sonja jumped right in, "Yes, actually, we've been sitting here talking most of the morning."

"Well, don't let me interrupt; I'm just here to change the linen. I won't be long."

The lingering look Matt gave her as he opened the door set her cheeks ablaze and she hurried inside. Each time she heard Sonja's high-pitched laughter, she pulled on the bed covers with unnecessary force. Finally, with the used sheets tucked under her arm, Amy opened the screen door when Sonja volunteered, "I've talked Matt into taking me out on the lake this afternoon. No sense sitting here and wasting this beautiful day."

Amy let the door bang shut behind her. "Sounds like a great idea." Amy looked into Matt's eyes and never flinched as she said, "I hear he enjoys escorting young women around the lake."

Matt offered no rebuttal. She'd gotten the last word. But somehow, Amy didn't feel victorious.

*   *   *

"What's ailing you, girl? You sick or somethin'? You're not the Amy I've known for two years."

Visualizing Matt and Sonja on the lake together was eating away at her, so much so that she had been short-tempered with Thelma when she asked her a simple question.

"I'm sorry, Thelma. Forgive me, please."

"Are you still worried about what that Evans man will say?"

"No. I'm resigned to the fact we have to sell. I don't have any control over that."

"Well, if it's not the lodge, and you're not sick, my intuition tells me you have a heart problem." Thelma's eyes twinkled above a smug smile.

"Excuse me? A heart problem?"

"Yep—the emotional kind. You won't admit it, but you're falling in love."

Amy's cheeks burst into flame as the emotion she'd been trying to hide rose to the surface. Was she really that transparent?

"Been there myself, you know. Charlie and I, rest his soul, would've been married thirty-five years next month. These past four years have been mighty lonely. Course, coming here to work has helped me get by. You aren't fooling this ole gal. I know it when I see it. I've got a feeling who it is, too."

"Have I been that obvious?" Tears spilled onto her freckled cheeks.

"Honey, I know you! It couldn't be Ted. You've said over and over 'he's a friend-period'. There's only one eligible male left. Matt."

Amy wiped at a tear and nodded her head.

"I'm so confused. I've never felt like this—not even with Eric. And I was engaged to him. This feeling is just so different."

"When love hits you, it hits hard, honey."

"Have you ever been jealous?"

"Jealous! Listen, my Charlie was one hunk of a man. His smile could melt your bones and I saw many a female wilt under my watchful eye. But he was faithful to me to the end. Why do you ask?"

"Sonja Newman. They've been gabbing all morning on his porch. Now, he's taken her out on the lake!"

"I thought you said she was coming onto Ted the other day."

"Until she met Matt."

"Amy, mark my words, he'll see through that little society gal and separate the wheat from the chaff. Men know the difference. Don't forget what he's been through."

Giving Thelma a hug, Amy confessed, "What would I do without you? Somehow you always manage to say the right thing—keep me centered. Are you sure you didn't come from Heaven?"

Chapter Thirteen

Amy changed her outfit three times before settling on a pair of white pants, a matching sleeveless top and red blazer. Satisfied with her refection in the mirror, she slipped her feet into sandals and skipped down the steps and into her father's office.

"Well, now," Henry asked, "where are you off to dressed like a million? Goin' to the city?"

"I am. There's not much to do around here today so I'm going to drive into North Bay and visit Mom awhile. Anything you want me to tell her?"

"The usual—I miss and love her. Course she knows that; but she needs to hear it a bunch these days. Tell her I'll be out to see her in a week or so."

"She's so lucky to have you, Daddy. Lots of men would've given up on her; but you've stuck by her side and seen her through some tough times." Amy hugged his neck. "I hope I'm as lucky some day."

Henry kissed Amy's cheek before continuing, "I know

getting over Eric's been tough, honey, but he wasn't for you. The right one will come along when you least expect it. You be careful on the highway; no lead foot, hear?"

"Promise," she called over her shoulder and headed toward the lake.

An hour and a half later Amy pulled into the parking lot of the rehabilitation center and made her way through the hallway to her mother's room. The doctor's instructions were implicit: "Keep things positive; no distressing news."

With the financial situation at the lodge worsening, Amy's stomach nerves twisted and churned each time she walked through the door. There was no way to predict her mom's roller coaster mood swings. Amy recalled how depressing the last visit had been with her mother crying and complaining that there was no purpose in her life. Other times a stranger would think she didn't have a care in the world. Bipolar personality described her mother to a T.

Amy offered a silent prayer, "Lord, please keep her on an even keel today."

"Hi, Mom." Amy's voice was light and cheery.

Emily Lawrence looked up from the book she'd been reading and walked over to embrace her daughter. "It's so good to see you, dear. My, I like that blazer. Red's your color—brings out the glow in your cheeks. I'm so relieved to see you looking perky again after that fiasco with what's-his-name."

"His name's Eric." She flicked a strand of hair behind her ear before continuing, "I'm ready to move on. He's past history."

"Thank goodness! Don't waste your time looking back or you could end up like me in a place like this."

"What do you mean?" Amy sighed as she recognized that depressing tone.

Emily took Amy's hand and led her to the sofa. "The doctors have been asking a lot of questions about my past and one of them thinks I have some regrets that were never

62

resolved."

"Regrets? Over what?"

"They think I envied my sisters and their city life-style while I worked at an isolated lodge for all these years. Burnout is the word Dr. Russell used. He tells me resentment can grow and fester for a long time until one day it erupts like a volcano."

For the first time, Amy felt the doctor might be on the right track. She'd recently come to a similar conclusion. No doubt business problems had pushed her mother over the edge.

Amy yearned to know more. "Is it true, Mom? Did you wish you'd stayed in Toronto?"

"At times. Especially when I was tied to the lodge, cooking, cleaning, trying to please every guest. My sisters were going places and doing exciting things. Then, these past couple years with business failing, I felt as though all my efforts were for nothing. I couldn't take it anymore." Tears spilled from weary eyes. "Now you have to fill my shoes."

Amy fought to keep her composure but went on, "What made you come back? You had a good job."

"Your father. Not that he forced me; he gave me a choice, but I loved him too much to stay away."

Amy longed to confess her feelings for Matt to her mother but it was too soon. She needed to know how he felt and so far he'd given no explanation for his kiss or his abrupt departure from the beach. Instead, she probed deeper, "Mom, how did you know it was love—real love? I can't make the same mistake I made with Eric. He blinded me with all his big talk and fancy ways."

Her mother smiled and a tenderness Amy hadn't seen in a long time enveloped Emily's face. "Somehow you just know. Your thoughts, spirit, and goals in life entwine in a way that will never unravel. Listen to your heart, Amy. And don't look back."

The two women hugged and as the lunch bell rang, Emily took her daughter's hand and said, "C'mon, I hear it's chicken salad today. I'm dying to know all the town gossip. Is it true Marge Bryant won a thousand dollars at the Legion bingo?"

Grateful that the moment of depression passed as quickly as it came, Amy did her best to keep her mother busy for the next few hours.

"I brought you that herbal shampoo you like, Mom. Let me wash your hair and style it so you're looking spiffy at dinner. I'll polish your nails, too."

"You know the nurses tell us when we look good, we feel good."

"They're right, Mom. I'll hem that new skirt you got and you can wear it tonight. You'll have them all wondering who the new woman is at the table."

Emily smiled. "Let's do it."

Before Amy realized it, the afternoon was gone and she needed to leave. She sighed with relief as she kissed her mother good-bye. She'd been able to steer their chit chat away from the financial problems—away from the reason a 'For Sale' sign was now part of Pine Lake Lodge. How long the reprieve would last was anyone's guess.

Chapter Fourteen

The Newmans' 'short' stay was turning into a week. On one of her cabin rounds to see if their guests were in need of anything, Amy heard Elaine exclaim, "We're all completely taken with this place. Why, Lyle hasn't had so much fun in years. The fishing's been great."

"He's had good luck, hasn't he?"

Without stopping for a breath, Elaine continued, "I'm finally getting a chance to catch up on my reading with no phone interruptions and Sonja hasn't complained once since we've been here. You know, just between you and me," she lowered her voice as if to reveal the strictest confidence, "I believe, that handsome Matt has a lot to do with it."

"Oh, really," Amy replied, fighting to control her reddening face, "He does seem to be an interesting guy, doesn't he?" Anxious to change the subject, she inquired, "Is there anything you need from town? One of us will be going in today."

"I don't believe so, dear. Ted, what a sweetheart, brought us groceries yesterday." With a book under one arm and a folding chair under the other, Elaine was off to the beach.

Later that afternoon, Henry returned from the village with a report that Benny would not be coming back for some time. The fracture was not healing to the doctor's satisfaction. Since he couldn't be much help at the lodge, his mother wanted him home to keep an eye on the younger children.

Henry's second announcement was more cheerful. "Read a poster at Jake's that should interest you, Amy. The annual wiener and corn roast is being held this Friday night. Been so preoccupied worrying about this place, it slipped my mind. You'll never guess where?" Henry continued before she could ask, "Right down the lake on Craig's Island."

"No kidding? Daddy, those parties are so much fun!"

"Think you'll go? You've had your nose to the grindstone all summer. I'll pass the word around to the folks here. They might enjoy it, you know. Somethin' different." With that, he was off to cabin seven.

Amy's mind was made up. She wouldn't miss one of the biggest social events of the summer. The tourists from the surrounding lakes always came, plus her friends from town. Her good spirits were bruised for a moment as she remembered that this year the locals were sure to outnumber the guests.

* * *

Friday dawned clear and bright. But then, it seemed to Amy that the weatherman always predicted the best of conditions for the annual corn roast. Smiling, Amy thought of the corn fields that probably got raided last night. The young folks meant no harm; the farmers expected it. They threw in some extra corn at planting time.

Morning chores kept Amy occupied. Problems with

the automatic washer forced her to bring out the old wringer-type. No fancy buttons to push on this one. It was pure physical labor from start to finish. Amy had to admit when it came to operating this antique, she was relieved the resort's laundry was light this summer.

At lunch Thelma flatly stated, "I have no intentions of climbing out of boats and over rocks in night as black as ink to sit on a log and burn a wiener."

"Thelma that's the fun of it!"

"At my age, I'm happy to sit on the dock with my fishing pole. And that's where I'm staying. This partying is for you young folks."

Thelma's lack of enthusiasm for the corn roast contrasted sharply with Sonja's bubbling anticipation. While waiting for the hanging sheets to dry, Amy had gone down to the lake for a swim and was preparing to dry off in the sun when Sonja spread her beach towel out beside her. "Isn't it exciting that they're having a town party while I'm here! To think we might have missed it, too."

"I rather doubt the whole town will turn out, Sonja."

"You know I've never been to a corn roast." Sonja ignored Amy's comment. "After all, you don't find that kind of stuff in the city. Handley Hills and a corn roast? I don't think so!" She chuckled softly. "You're going I presume?"

She wasn't about to give Sonja any satisfaction. "I may; not sure."

"Well, I finally talked Matt into taking me. He was reluctant at first. I think it was because of his leg, but I won him over. Mom and Dad are staying home. Not much for the party scene."

Amy had heard all she wanted to hear. She jumped up and grabbed her towel. "I have to go. Thelma needs me in the kitchen."

Fuming, she thumped up the stone steps. Her mind was made up. No way would she go to the corn roast alone, knowing Matt and Sonja would be there together. Thelma would have company tonight after all.

Since Amy changed her plans, there was no need to hurry with the evening dishes and cleanup. As she stood at the sink, scrubbing pots and pans, she looked out the window and saw a number of boats filled with passengers headed for Craig's Island. One of the boats was Ted's. But instead of traveling on, it turned in toward the lodge. About the time Ted stepped from his boat, Thelma called to Amy, "Aren't you ready to join all those folks?"

"I'm not going."

"What brought this on?"

"A blond with a loose tongue."

"Eh? Sounds interesting. Go on."

"Sonja told me that Matt was taking her."

Before Thelma could respond, Ted knocked at the door.

Amy called out to him, "If you're looking for Sonja, she isn't here."

"Where is she?"

"On the island."

Ted looked surprised and asked, "Did she go herself?"

"Oh, no, she's in good company. Matt took her."

Seeing the disappointment in Amy's eyes, Thelma interrupted, "Amy needs a ride."

"I told you…"

Thelma cut her off, "Where's that fighting spirit, Hon? Show her a thing or two."

A smile crinkled the corners of Amy's mouth as she turned to Ted. "I was just going to change. Won't be long. Is second best o.k. with you?"

"Since when have I ever considered you second best? Get a move on, girl."

Chapter Fifteen

In less than thirty minutes, Amy sat on the bow of Ted's boat watching the reflection of the huge bonfire dancing on the surrounding water. Boats were tied to any old log that would hold them, and the melodious sounds of laughter echoed from boat to shore. For the next few hours Craig's Island would be this party crowd's playground.

Sonja was easy to spot in the sea of familiar faces formed around the fire. The glow of the flames enhanced the gold in her hair. One hand was linked around Matt's arm while the other held a long stick with a wiener dangling precariously over a burning log.

Everyone shifted around until Ted and Amy were sitting opposite Matt and Sonja, she flashed them a teasing smile, allowing it to linger for a long moment on Ted.

Amy wanted to gag. Matt simply nodded his head in their direction, but he wasn't paying Sonja much attention either, focusing rather on his conversation with the couple next to him. Once his gazed traveled across the shooting flames to Amy and their eyes met and held. He blinked first and turned back to the couple, leaving her confused, but intrigued. Before long, someone in the crowd produced a guitar, and a whispering breeze carried away the sounds of voices singing old and new songs. Meanwhile, the flames of the fire burned down to cherry-red coals just perfect for boiling corn. An old, scorched washtub, battle-scarred from many past occasions, half filled with water sat on the coals. Husked, pale cobs simmered in the boiling water for ten minutes until each kernel turned golden.

Mouths watered and lips smacked as everyone bit into succulent juices until all appetites were satisfied and a mound of discarded naked cobs, ready to be thrown into the fire, grew higher. Two local teens removed the washtub and added more logs to the fire. While most sat back and watched the rainbow of colors in the dancing flames, occasionally, a couple would slip away from the circle into the shelter of darkness.

Sonja leaned close to Matt and whispered in his ear, then stood up and went over to Ted. Placing one hand on his shoulder, she bent down and said, "I know I can't find my way to the boat, Ted, and I'd like my sweater. Matt left his light in the boat. Will you show me the way?"

Amy stifled the laugh that choked in her throat as she saw right through Sonja's scheme. *So Matt isn't giving you the attention you expected. Hmm ... bored already, eh?*

But apparently Ted wasn't bored. The words were barely out of Sonja's mouth when he jumped up, took her by the hand, and together they went to the boats. Matt waited until they were out of sight, then stood up and walked around to where Amy was seated. She sensed his towering presence above her before he spoke.

"Mind if I sit?"

"Make yourself comfortable."

Matt inched his body down onto the log. Amy could feel the pressure of his arm against hers as he sat close.

"I haven't seen you the past few days. Where've you been?"

Amy was tempted to tell him that with Sonja monopolizing his time, it didn't surprise her he hadn't noticed much.

"Taking care of Benny's chores—plus my own."

"Amy, I have to ask you something." His look was penetrating. "Have you been avoiding me?"

She hadn't expected this honesty. Her mind spun. How could she tell Matt she was in love with him? That each time she saw him with another woman it drove her crazy?

Relief swept through her when he didn't wait for an answer but went on, "I was afraid that maybe I'd stepped out of line at the beach."

The moment of truth had come and she mustered the courage to ask, "Matt why did you...?" Suddenly, a piercing cry stopped Amy in mid-sentence. Startled, everyone jumped up and ran toward its origin.

Sonja lay on the ground whimpering, "My ankle. It hurts! It hurts!"

Desperately trying to comfort her and locate the injury at the same time, Ted only made things worse. Sonja continued to cry out, "It hurts. Oh, where's Matt? I need Matt."

Appearing from the shadows, Matt tried to calm her down.

The sobs and quivering voice continued, "It's broken, I know it!"

Matt examined the injury while someone assisted with a bright light.

"No broken bones; you probably twisted it."

His examination did little to reassure her and she insisted, "Take me home, Matt. I can't stay here in pain."

Before Matt could answer, Ted began apologizing, "Gee, Sonja, I'm sorry. I thought you had a hold of me. Here, put your arms around my neck and let me carry you to the boat."

Matt started to follow then turned and stepped back beside Amy. He leaned close to her ear and whispered, "We need to talk."

By now, the party was beginning to break up, although there were a few diehards determined to see the last embers fade. Amy wasn't one of them. When Ted returned from the shoreline she suggested they leave.

"Amy, I don't understand it," Ted said as they walked to his boat. "I had my arm around her, and we almost reached you and Matt when her body went limp and down she went."

"I guess she's just a fragile little thing." Her sarcasm went unnoticed by Ted, but Amy knew the truth. It was just another one of Sonja's ploys to separate Matt and her. Wait 'til Thelma heard this one.

Chapter Sixteen

Dreams of last night's corn roast were fresh in her memory, especially Matt's conversation. Was it possible that he cared for her, too?

The ringing telephone brought her back to reality. She heard a door slam, running footsteps, and Thelma's breathless hello. Amy was fastening the last button on her shirt when Thelma called up the stairs, "Jamie's on the line. He's coming to see your father later this afternoon and wants to know if you need anything from town."

"Just the mail."

Thelma was back at her chores by the time Amy entered the kitchen. The smell of freshly perked deep-roasted coffee hung in the air. Amy poured a cup then sat at the table. She knew Thelma was dying to know what happened at the corn roast. Amy spared no details. When she came to Sonja's performance, Thelma's eyes grew larger and her interest deepened.

"So she managed to be center-stage after all."

"I know it was nothing more than an act to separate Matt and me. I'd bet my last dime she's faking it."

"There'll always be women like that. At least with the hussies they're straight forward with what they want. But it's the helpless, sweet-talking honeys you can't trust. They'll do anything to get a man's attention. But I can't believe Matt isn't smart enough to see through her schemes. He doesn't strike me as anybody's fool."

Amy took another sip of coffee. "I guess we'll find out, now won't we?"

* * *

Waves from Jamie's twin-hulled Sea Spray crashed against the shoreline as he pulled up to the dock and called, "Hi cousin. Loafing again I see."

Amy looked up from the flower bed she was weeding. "Just you get over here and see the fruits of my labor."

"Looks good. Adds a nice touch." Jamie was a good natured, likeable fellow who rolled with the punches.

"Do you think Canadian Uranium will appreciate the floral display? I'm sure the local grapevine reached your ears, too."

"I heard a mining company was interested in the place, if that's what you mean?"

"We don't like the idea, but it seems the only answer. Mom's hospital bills aren't getting any smaller, and I don't have to remind you what it costs to run a fishing lodge."

"Spare me the agony. Karen and I are just hanging in there. With the new baby due soon, we'll be having a few extra bills ourselves. Say, what was the name of that mining outfit?"

"Canadian Uranium."

"Look in that pile of mail." Jamie handed Amy a plain brown bag filled with letters and magazines. "It just hit me. I believe I saw that name on an envelope when I was getting the mail."

Nervously, Amy fingered through the stack of letters.

74

She stopped at the fourth, pulled it out and read the return address. Jamie was right. Canadian Uranium had sent their reply. What would it be? Either way, Amy felt defeated. If the company bought the lodge, everything this place meant to her would be lost forever. If they voted against it, the future held financial ruin. Right now, the game of life seemed like a stacked deck to her. She swallowed hard to keep down the lump in her throat. Tears wouldn't help. Her mind was made up; she had to be strong. Her father didn't need two depressed women on his hands and there was no telling how her mother would take the news.

At that moment, Henry, coming from the boathouse, called out to Jamie, "Hello there. Thought that was your boat at the dock. What's up?"

"Uncle Henry, do you still have that canoe for sale you were telling me about? I'd like to take a look at it."

"Sure, it's rolled over on the beach. Hardly a scratch on it. Go on over and see for yourself."

"This came today," Amy said as Jamie struck off on his mission. She handed Henry the long white envelope.

At first glance, he saw it was from the mining company. "They weren't long in getting back to us, were they?" His pocket knife slit the end of the envelope.

A moment of tension passed between them. As they caught each other's eye, Amy sensed what the letter contained. Only the sentence, 'We accept your terms...', registered in Amy's mind as Henry read it aloud. When he finished, Amy squeezed her father's hand and said, "You did what you had to do."

Henry nodded "This means Evans and I will have to meet at the lawyer's office next week to sign the final papers."

There didn't seem to be much more to say, so Henry went to join Jamie while Amy trudged up the hill to the lodge to tell Thelma the news. She leafed through the remaining letters. There was a postcard from a friend on vacation, a piece of junk mail, another bill, and a letter addressed to Matt. In her nervousness over the mining company, Amy hadn't noticed it. Feeling a little guilty, she read the return address. It was none of her business but the name looked familiar. Then she remembered mailing a letter to Dr. Robert Monroe for Matt a week ago. Since Matt received an answer so quickly, Amy decided it must be important and took it right over.

Matt's boat was gone and the cottage door was closed. Amy was stepping off the last step when Sonja called from her porch, "He's fishing with my father. Would you like me to deliver a message?"

"No thanks. I'll catch him when he gets back."

"Suit yourself," she replied swinging her injured foot in the air to dry the newly polished toenails.

*   *   *

With a little coaxing from Thelma, Jamie stayed for supper. Everyone traded tidbits of local gossip as the meal progressed. The men discussed fishing, the best it'd been in years. Such a shame more visitors couldn't enjoy it. As usual, the recent weather conditions entered the conversation. All agreed the summer was extremely dry and rain was needed. No one discussed Canadian Uranium.

While washing the dishes, Amy noticed Matt's boat return. She would have taken the letter to him as soon as the kitchen was cleaned, but a call from a relative held her up. After several attempts to end the conversation, Amy finally placed the receiver back in its cradle. She picked up the letter, stole a glance in the mirror, and started toward Matt's cottage. A full moon spread a carpet of light on the trail before her. Would this be the night he continued their conversation and answered her question? She hoped so.

However, her hopes shattered the closer she got to cabin eight as the sound of splashing water and laughing voices broke the silence. She knew at once it was Sonja and Matt standing on the dock. Beads of water reflected off their bodies in the moonlight.

"Excuse me, sorry to interrupt." She stepped onto the dock and waited. Matt turned to face Amy, picked up a towel and walked closer.

"Sorry, I didn't see you. The water feels great after a day in the blistering sun. Why don't you join us?"

"No thanks, I just came down to give you this." She handed Matt the letter.

"It's probably from my dad. I've been expecting to hear from him."

Amy turned to go but once again Matt touched her arm and insisted, "Sure you won't change your mind. The water's great!"

Sonja was quick to interject, "She's probably dead on her feet, Matt. You know how hard she works around here." With that, she gave a little bounce and dove into the lake.

Sprained ankle, eh?, Pretty fast recovery! Angry and deflated, Amy returned to the lodge.

Chapter Seventeen

Sleep hadn't come easily. The rumpled linen on Amy's bed was proof that she'd tossed and turned most of the night. In her dreams she kept running and running until she was totally exhausted. She sat up and shook her head in hopes the grogginess would disappear. No luck. She decided a cold shower was the answer. The pulsating spray of the water shot little pellets of life back into her fatigued body.

While she was drying off, Amy decided she needed to get away from the lodge for a few hours. She wanted to think—get a grip on her feelings. But where could she go? A trip to town didn't excite her; a visit to one of the other lodges would be depressing, as the conversation, no doubt, would turn to the news that Pine Lake Lodge was up for sale. Besides, she wanted to be alone.

Then it came to her. Why not go down to their old raspberry patch and make herself useful. No one would bother her and the thought of a sweet, juicy berry pie for supper was the deciding vote.

She dressed in jeans, a long-sleeved shirt and sneakers. It might be warm, but raspberry bushes showed no mercy when it came to bare arms and legs.

Downstairs, she told Thelma her plans as she poured a bowl of cereal.

"Where on earth are you going? Your father's already left for town. Said he had to get a bundle of shingles to repair a couple roofs before he sells."

"It looks like you'll be holding down the fort by yourself. I'm going about two miles down the lake."

"Bless you, girl. My mouth's been watering for a pie all week. I picked a few by the fence and they are so good."

"We've always gotten plenty. There's an old logging road that goes into the woods for miles. You know, that's the perfect spot for raspberries to grow."

"Be careful now. I wish Benny were here to go with you. Do you really think you should go alone? I don't suppose you'd ask Sonja to go with you?"

"Are you kidding?" Amy almost dropped her spoon. "I've seen enough of her these past few days." Amy continued, "Last night when I went down to give Matt his letter, I found the two of them enjoying a moonlight swim. Matt invited me to join them but Sonja let me know I wasn't welcome."

"O.K. Bad idea. Go by yourself, but listen. The weatherman is calling for rain this afternoon. Lord only knows we need it. Do you think you'll be back by then?"

"I should be. I can only handle a couple of pails at a time. Rain, eh? Maybe it will cool my attitude. It was pretty hot last night!"

*   *   *

Within fifteen minutes, Amy's boat was speeding effortlessly over the waves. The refreshing breeze in her face cleared the morning's cobwebs and the blue sky overhead did not look ominous. She shielded her eyes from the sun's glare with the palm of her hand as she scanned the shoreline for a place to secure the boat. A small, quiet bay suggested a natural harbor, so Amy turned in and cut back on the throttle. Here the boat would be spared the continual rocking against a ragged shoreline.

Amy tied the rope to a fallen tree, felled by the work of some industrious beaver. Satisfied that her craft would stay put, she started off to find the logging road. Each year, it was harder to find. Finally, her sense of smell led her to the ripe, lush, red raspberries. They hung in clusters, their weight bending the bushes to the ground. It wasn't hard to visualize one of Thelma's baked pies.

While Amy picked berry after berry, little birds chirped in the branches overhead. Chipmunks scampered from tree to tree chattering and scolding. She was an intruder; the forest was their domain and trespassers weren't appreciated. Unwelcome as she might be, Amy felt at peace among the wildlife. Nature provided all their needs. Branches loaded with greenery stretched out from the maple trees like giant arms offering protection from the elements. A soft bed of moss and decomposed leaves lay on the forest floor, concealing any number of insects to whet the tiniest bird's appetite. The scent of wintergreen lingered in the air. Nothing was complicated here.

Within forty-five minutes, Amy filled a five-pound shortening can with berries. At this rate, it would be no trouble to fill the second. She decided to leave the first pail on a tree stump and pick it up on her return. No point in carrying the extra load--it would just be in the way.

The sun climbed higher as Amy wandered deeper into the woods. The position of the road became more difficult to define. New saplings and thick berry bushes appeared to spring up in front of her. A quick glance over her shoulder told Amy she needed to pay close attention to where she'd been in order to find her way back to the lake.

Beads of perspiration ran down her forehead and

cheeks. It suddenly felt very warm. Wiping her flushed face with the back of her sleeve, she sat down to rest. She hadn't intended to wander this far from the lake, but each new berry bush offered larger and juicier berries than the last.

If it hadn't been for the shrill screaming of a blue jay, Amy wouldn't have noticed the change in the sky. Looking up, she saw a bird flying against a yellowish-gray background, not the pale blue seen earlier.

"That's strange," thought Amy, "the storm clouds must be moving in faster than predicted."

Deciding it was best to start home, she picked up her pail and turned back. She heard it again—more screaming birds! Something was bothering them. A gust of wind brought the startling truth. Amy smelled smoke! Forest fire! Careless campers? Heat lightening?

For a second, her mind froze. Which way should she go? Everything looked the same. She had to concentrate on the lake. She ran through the bushes, thorns tearing at her shirt, berries spilling in all directions. In frustration, she threw the pail by the wayside. She didn't have time to stop and figure where the road lay. She'd have to rely on her instincts.

The smoke was all around her now. It lodged in her throat as she gasped for breath. Water-filled eyes blurred her vision. She became confused. By her calculations, she should have reached the stump where she left the first pail of berries. Frightened animals came out of nowhere. Rabbits outraced her; she saw the flash of a deer's tail and lumbering behind him was a porcupine. Amy was no longer the threat.

Behind them a crashing tree sent sparks soaring everywhere and she heard the snapping and crackling of burning bush. In all this turmoil, Amy had a dreadful thought. What if the wind carried this inferno to the lodge? To be wiped out by fire just when the mining company was ready to buy would be the final blow!

Pain from the smoke and constant gasping welled up in her chest. Her throat felt like parchment and her legs began to wobble. She knew she was lost. Blurring tears ran down her cheeks. She lost her footing and met the forest floor with a thud dashing her right temple against the jagged edge of a tree root. She lay there, in a state of absolute exhaustion, as blood oozed from the small, deep cut.

Was that a roar she heard? Amy listened. Yes, it was a roar—a constant roar. Only the dam with its white foamy water cascading over the concrete and hitting the boulders below had that distinct, familiar sound. She'd been running in the wrong direction, but there was no going back. She had no choice but to go forward. Staggering to her feet, a sudden jolt of adrenaline propelled her onward. The forest appeared to open up before her as the thundering grew louder.

Amy prayed as she clawed and pulled at every branch and shrub that the dam lay over the approaching knoll. At last, weak and trembling, she reached the top. Her swollen eyes filled with tears of relief. Foamy, white water plunged over the rocks below as if applauding Amy's efforts to find safety. With no hesitation, she tumbled down the hill to the shoreline, submerging her fiery face into the refreshing oasis. The coolness of the water cleared her head and she knew where she was in relation to the boat. Her only recourse was to follow the shoreline back about a mile.

Before starting the trek, she rolled on her back and watched clouds of gray smoke mixed with cinders and ash drift out over the lake. She fought the temptation to stay and rest but pure will forced her to start moving again.

Though the shoreline was safer than going back into the woods, the footing was worse. Loose rocks threatened her unsteady legs and several times she slipped, jarring her ankles.

Another familiar sound caught her attention and she looked up through the drifting gray fumes to see the red and white ranger plane circling the lake. "Thank you," she cried in praise, her voice cracking in pain. She knew it carried enough equipment and men to get the fire-fighting team started. Then, depending on the wind, the plane would dump water on the flames.

Her boat was in sight now—not only Amy's, but, three others as well. Relief washed over her battered body. Inching her way closer, she recognized two boats belonging to the rangers. The third was Ted's.

She tried to yell but no words were audible. One of the rangers looked in her direction and saw her stumbling over fallen logs and craggy rocks. He pointed her out to two other men who immediately yelled at the top of their lungs, "Stay there! We're coming!"

There was no contest between Ted and Matt. With his red hair flying in all directions, Ted leaped from one rock to another until he reached his goal. Several yards back, Matt, determined to master each obstacle, called out, "Don't move her. Wait 'till I get there."

Ted had Amy's head resting against his shoulder when Matt, seeing her wound, whipped off his shirt and dipped it into the water. He gently wiped a mixture of dirt, blood and sweat from her face. He determined the lesion was superficial. No stitches needed.

Amy tried to talk but the effort was fruitless. Her body ached all over and her blood-red eyes were visible only through tiny slits.

The constant drone of the outboard motor kept her from falling into a deep sleep. She fought to stay awake. Vaguely, Amy remembered Ted carrying her to the lodge and placing her on the sofa. Bits and pieces of conversation drifted around in her head. She heard Thelma's frantic concern. "I told her not to go alone." Was that Matt talking to Dr. Willis? And what was pounding on the roof—rain? Yes, rain, blessed rain.

The last thing Amy remembered was the sweetest

memory of all. A soothing hand stroked the tangled strands of smoke-filled hair away from her face and Matt whispered close to her ear, "Amy, you're home. Safe now. You need to rest but I'll be right here beside you."

She was sure she felt a feather-like touch of his lips on her forehead. She offered a faint smile as sleep came at last.

Chapter Eighteen

The fire was out. Charred stumps, fallen, scarred trees, and the smell of burnt grass lingered in the air as a grim reminder of the fire's menacing power.

Amy needed little to remind her of yesterday's threat.

Her entire body ached. Enflamed leg muscles smarted each time she twitched her toes. Vocal chords, irritated by constant smoke inhalation, produced a harsh edge to the sound of her voice. The facial wound, although red, was no longer swollen.

Thelma volunteered to serve Amy breakfast in bed, but she insisted on showering, dressing and eating downstairs. Besides, she had questions-lots of questions.

Henry walked into the kitchen as his daughter sat down at the table. He walked over and gave her shoulders a squeeze.

"How's my girl this morning?" Before Amy could respond, he went on, "About gave your ole dad a heart attack yesterday, honey. I was pickin' up some shingles and that Matthews kid came a'runnin' into the store yellin' that a fire had been spotted not too far from us. Then I get home and find out you're in it! Mercy!" Henry wiped his brow and shook his head from side to side.

"I walked into it all right. That was the easy part. Getting away was another story. The old logging road isn't there anymore. The raspberry bushes have taken it over. I should've used more sense than to wander back so far but the berries sure were plentiful. And to think, after all that, I didn't even bring one home. Left the pails out there, too."

Thelma couldn't contain herself," My word, girl. Who cares about the berries? I was a nervous wreck worrying about you wandering around by yourself."

Amy flashed her an appreciative smile. "I'm sorry, Thelma. Didn't mean to upset you. I sure was surprised to see Matt and Ted. How did they know where to find me?"

"The rangers told me a couple fellows fishing down by the big rock saw the smoke and reported it to the tower. You know the routine when there's an emergency. They start calling everyone on the lake to warn them."

"That's when I called Ted," continued Thelma. "Told him you'd gone off in that direction and your father was in town. He wanted me to find Matt. Guess he figured he might need his medical experience. Anyway, Matt was eating lunch when I told him the news. Didn't waste a second. He was waiting on the dock when Ted swung in to pick him up."

"Matt showed a lot of concern for you, Amy," said Henry. "He stayed here until almost midnight and we had a long talk. He's seen the rough side of life, too. But he seems to have a smart head on his shoulders. Runs the business end of his father's medical clinic."

Amy remembered the return address on the letter she delivered to Matt and asked, "So, his father is a doctor?"

"Specializes in handicapped patients, especially veterans. Matt says his own injury has had a lot to do with his dad's interest in helping vets. I'm thankful this young man was here to help us this summer."

"I couldn't agree more, Daddy."

Unaware of the secret Amy held in her heart, Henry continued, "I believe he has foresight. Knows a good deal when he sees one."

"What does that mean?"

"Oh, just an observation."

Amy dug deeper, "You're holding back on me, Daddy. That's not like you. You know I'll find out sooner than later."

"Then it'll have to be later. I'm taking Lyle Newman out fishing." He was gone before Amy could pry any further.

* * *

By lunch, Amy had read several magazines, manicured her nails, and answered an overdue letter. Now she was bored. It wasn't her style to sit around doing nothing. If she tried to do the simplest chore, Thelma pounced on her like a watchdog. She closed her eyes and lay back in the lounge chair. Putting the drama she'd experienced out of her mind was difficult. It played over and over. Each time she imagined hearing the sound of crackling burning brush, her heart beat faster. She wondered how long before this feeling faded from memory. Perhaps it would disappear faster if she concentrated on the present. The thought of Matt brought a smile but then there was Sonja.

Not a second passed before Amy's reverie was shattered by an accusing voice, "My, my, but some people will go to extremes for attention, now won't they? Really, getting caught in a forest fire!"

Amy's eyes popped open. Coming toward her in a pale blue jogging suit was Sonja. Panting behind was her mother.

"Now, Sonja, that wasn't a nice thing to say," Elaine scolded.

"Oh, Mother, Amy knows I'm only kidding."

"I'm sure it was a compliment," Amy paused before continuing, "Coming from an expert."

Amy hit a hot spot. The corners of Sonja's mouth dropped as her smile disappeared. Her eyes grew intense and bore into Amy's.

"Well, you certainly caught our neighbor's attention last night. It was midnight before he came back to his cabin."

"If you're referring to Matt, he spent the evening talking to my father. I collapsed with exhaustion—hardly able to entertain anyone."

Elaine broke the tension. "Well, dear, we're all thankful they found you in time. It could've been so much worse. Take care and rest, sweetie. Sonja, are you ready for another lap?"

Amy watched as mother and daughter broke into stride. She knew she should've ignored Sonja's caustic remark, but the temptation to do verbal battle with her was too much. In the future, Amy promised to hold her tongue. But then, she smiled, promises can be broken.

Chapter Nineteen

Amy answered one phone call after another all evening. The local grapevine was abuzz with details——not all of them true. Friends and relatives wanted to know firsthand if she really was encircled by flames and how badly was her leg burned? After setting the record straight and reassuring everyone she was going to recover, she finally placed the receiver back on its hook for the fifth time. On the sixth call, she sighed aloud, "Oh, no, I refuse to answer. If I have to tell one more person how it feels to be chased by a forest fire ..."

The ringing was persistent. Giving in, she picked up the receiver but her lack of enthusiasm was obvious.

"Hello."

"May I speak to Mr. Lawrence, please?"

The voice was not familiar, but Amy knew she'd heard it before.

Her lethargy disappeared and she responded politely, "One moment, please, and I'll get him. May I ask who's calling?"

"Tom Evans."

Now she knew. The voice belonged to the Canadian Uranium representative.

As she walked to the porch to get her father, Amy felt the inevitable. No doubt, the company was ready to sign the final papers. She lowered her voice and spoke through the screen door, "Tom Evans, Canadian Uranium on the phone for you, Daddy." Henry wasted no time in taking the call.

No longer needed, Amy sat on the porch. She wasn't eavesdropping, however, Henry's voice drifted out through the screen door and into the night air.

"Yes, I received your letter, two, three days ago, Tom." A short pause followed before Henry continued, "You'll be coming up north this week. Yes, I can meet you Thursday morning, ten o'clock at the Lakeview Motel. We can drive into North Bay in an hour and a half. It's seventy miles from here." Another short pause. "Oh, yes, my lawyer will have a purchase agreement drawn up. I do, however, have a matter to discuss with you before we do any signing, Tom."

Hearing this, Amy wondered if her father was having a change of heart. She tried to imagine what could put a stop to this deal. They had discussed the pros and cons of selling to the mining company. Painful as it might be, the final decision had been made to sell.

"I'll be looking forward to seeing you then, Tom. I appreciate the call. Goodnight."

Amy made no attempt to pry into the matter. Whatever her father had to discuss with Tom Evans was his affair. This time, she decided to stay out of it.

Chapter Twenty

"An overnight camping trip!"

The excitement in Thelma's voice caught Amy's attention. "Who's going camping?"

"Would you believe Mr. Newman wants your father to take all three of them?" Thelma continued to rant in disbelief, "Can't you see those women curled up in a musty old sleeping bag! Long way from a Beauty Rest, Honey."

"Now, now, Thelma," Henry said, "don't be too hard on them. It's been years since Lyle has been able to do anything like this. Elaine's a good sport to go along with him. How 'bout you, Amy? Care to come? I could use your help with the cooking."

"Sure, I'll go. I love to camp. Remember how mom used to cook those special pancakes over the open fire?"

"Melt in your mouth, especially, with pure maple syrup on them. Hmm, I can taste them now. Say, thought I'd ask Matt to join us. Believe he'd enjoy seeing some new territory."

Amy's breath quickened. This could prove interesting.

"Are you sure you feel up to this, young lady?" Thelma's concern was genuine. "If memory serves me correctly, you had to be carried home not more than three days ago."

"Just try and keep me at home," Amy teased, "and you'll see how well I've recuperated."

"I concede. You win."

"I wonder if Ted could spare the time," mused Henry. "He knows Swan Lake pretty well. Besides, we could use that boat he keeps over there. I'll give him a call."

Amy knew this sort of activity was born and bred in her father. She saw the gleam in his eye and the excitement in his voice as he prepared for this camping trip as eagerly as any young boy.

The preparations took most of the morning. Henry rummaged through the storehouse until the tent, sleeping bags, Coleman lantern and stove were located. Thelma insisted upon baking fresh cookies, tarts, and bread for the gang while Amy gathered utensils, canned staples, and the all-important iron skillet. A quick call to Ted confirmed that he'd be at the lodge by three o'clock.

Amy packed lightly since a two-mile portage was part of the trip. Her backpack contained the vital necessities: towel, change of clothes, hairbrush, toothbrush, and toilet paper. However, as she stepped onto the main dock, she saw that the Newman women must have thought they were going for a week. The smile on her face was close to a snicker when Henry suggested to Elaine that she wouldn't have time for her needlepoint.

Sonja was quick to notice Amy and her backpack. "You don't intend to come with us, do you?"

Before Amy could answer, Lyle cut in, "Of course, she's coming. Why shouldn't she?"

"Three days ago the girl could barely walk. I'd think anyone suffering from exhaustion would have the common sense to take it easy."

"We Canadian women recover quickly, Sonja." Her smile was self-assured. "Somethin' in the air, they tell me. Apparently, it works. Don't you agree?"

The battle lines were drawn already and they hadn't left the dock yet.

Sonja seated herself beside Matt, Ted was driving the boat, so that left Amy to sit on the bow. Henry, Lyle and Elaine took the larger supply craft.

Sonja's constant chatter kept the attention of the two men. Amy appreciated the obvious exclusion as it gave her the opportunity to face the wind, close her eyes and inhale the tingling fresh air. After her recent experience in the fire, this simple act was sheer pleasure.

A half hour went by before the boats headed for shore. Jutting out into the water lay a weather-beaten dock. Here and there a broken board spelled danger. The first thing Elaine did when she got out of the boat was lose her balance and step into a gaping hole, scraping her left shin. More startled than hurt, she was a good sport and was ready to continue. Amy felt certain, had it been Sonja, the camping trip would have come to a screeching halt!

Winding into the woods was a trail about three feet wide. Henry explained that they would walk single file.

"You mean we aren't camping here?" asked Elaine.

"No dear, we have to walk two miles," replied Lyle. "Remember, I told you the campsite is on another lake."

"We have to carry all this stuff?" Sonja was not thrilled. "Father, what have you gotten us into? No one mentioned a marathon hike!"

"And just what do you think a portage is, Sonja?" Lyle was losing his patience.

"Well, thank heavens I wore the right shoes."

While Sonja and Lyle sparred with each other, Amy helped the men unload the boats. She'd heard the cliché 'blonds have more fun' but were they all this naive?

Ted volunteered to carry an outboard motor, so he took the lead. Usually, Henry hoisted it upon his shoulders, but Amy was pleased to see that today he wouldn't have to carry the extra load. He had enough burdens to handle these days. Everyone picked up a share of gear and fell into line. Each person looked like a pack mule carrying fishing rods, sleeping bags, food supplies and personal belongings.

Mosquitoes lay in wait as the party walked deeper into the woods. Their monotone humming gave fair warning; then came the attack. Sonja and Elaine discovered that expensive perfume not only attracts those of the opposite sex, but also draws pesky insects. Deep Woods insect repellent soon became the favored fragrance of the day.

Halfway through the portage, Sonja called a halt. "I can't go another step," her breathing was raspy.

"For someone who jogs every morning, you haven't much to show for it," commented Lyle.

"Father, I don't carry half a ton on my back and swat these blood-thirsty insects!"

Henry stepped in and apologized, "I'm sorry, Sonja, I was setting my own pace. I keep forgetting that everyone isn't used to this type of life. How 'bout a five –minute stop?"

"Oh, I'll second that," said Elaine. "This is a little different than running around our block."

Everyone agreed to a rest, all except Ted. There was no stopping him once he started—-not with the weight of an outboard on his shoulders.

Amy looked at Matt. Was he finding the going too rough? His load was equal to his companions, but his relaxed manner eased her mind. Then she remembered, it was rigorous physical therapy that put him on his feet again.

Staying in one spot too long gave the mosquitoes a direct advantage, so with little hesitation Sonja and Elaine moved on. The last half of the portage was easier as it sloped down to the lake and a light breeze kept the bugs away.

Swan Lake stretched out before them like a rare jewel. Sapphire water lay surrounded by emerald evergreens. The beauty of the area did not go unnoticed as Lyle remarked, "Oh, my! Now this was worth a two-mile hike."

"Fantastic!" was Matt's reaction. "Say, Henry, how's the fishing here? I bet the bass are waiting for that new spoon you showed me."

"Well, why don't you take Lyle and go find out. There's no time like the present."

"Go ahead, Matt," Ted called from the boat where he had secured the motor. "I'm going to help Henry set up camp."

"Wait for me," Sonja shouted. It was apparent she was not going to be any help.

"Come in when you're hungry," Amy directed her words to Matt. "I'll have something cooking."

"Sounds great, Amy." Once again his smile triggered a warm, throbbing sensation throughout her body.

"Well, I hope it's good," butted in Sonja, "We probably should've talked Thelma into coming."

Amy ignored her remark. She turned her back and started to pull cooking utensils out of the pack. Feeling a hand on her shoulder, Amy looked up into Ted's face.

"Don't let her get to you. It's plain to see she's a whiny, spoiled brat. You know you can run rings around her."

"Oh, I let her sarcastic remarks go in one ear and out the other. I'm surprised you had your eyes opened, though."

"It's not hard to see through a girl like her. All you have to do is listen. You've heard the way she talks to her parents—not much respect. I've a feeling life has pretty much centered around Sonja, and she doesn't like it when the attention is on someone else. My guess is that Matt would agree."

"Oh, I'm not so sure about that." Amy's face turned pink. She hadn't intended her feelings to show.

"You care for that guy, don't you?"

Her smile said it all.

"Amy," Ted lowered his voice, "you know you've always been special to me."

"Ted, we've talked about this…"

He held up his hand in a halting gesture cutting her off, "Now listen. I realized when you got involved with Eric that ours was a platonic relationship. But just for the record, I didn't shed any tears when you broke up with him. The guy's a jerk!"

"I'll second that!"

"Now Matt, in my opinion is a winner. Hang in there; be patient. It'll work out."

"I hope you're right, Ted. Thanks." Amy reached over and squeezed his hand.

Chapter Twenty-one

Slowly, the campsite took shape. Henry and Ted erected the all-weather tent beneath some towering pines, Amy gathered wood and stacked it on a rock plateau in readiness for the evening fire, and Elaine propped the rods and nets against some spruce trees.

Satisfied that things were in order, Henry and Ted picked up their fishing gear and started out to try their luck.

"Where've you got that canoe hidden, Henry?"

"Look to your right, just over that knoll. I keep it here during the summer. Saves me haulin' it back to the lodge every time I come over here."

"Canoe! Oh, Henry, it's been years since I've ridden in a canoe," Elaine slammed the pages of the book she'd been reading together and jumped out of her chair. "Please take me along."

A doubtful expression crossed Ted's face. "Gee, Elaine, it's kind of small and not all that steady."

"I promise not to budge, Ted."

The pleading in her voice was enough for Henry. He gave in.

"You'll have to sit in the middle, flat on the bottom. And remember, no fancy maneuvers."

"You're the boss, Skipper," her laugh was on the verge of hyper. "I can't wait 'til Lyle sees this!"

Ted shook his head from side to side. He muttered to himself all the way to the shoreline, but Elaine was too excited to notice.

With everyone gone, Amy basked in the solitude. Now and again the silence was broken by Elaine's squeals of delight. From what Amy had witnessed earlier, Sonja wasn't the only one in the Newman family used to getting her own way.

As the sun started its decline, Amy began preparation for dinner. She was taking the container marked beef stew out of the food box when she heard Elaine yell, "Get the net! Get the net! He's huge!"

Not far from the campsite, Ted struggled with a northern pike. It thrashed against the side of the canoe and then dove under it taking several yards of line with him. Each time this happened, Elaine grew more excited. She twisted from side to side, sending the canoe into a roll and Ted into a frenzy.

"Elaine, take it easy! You'll have us all swimming home."

The words were scarcely out of his mouth when the pike took another dive and Elaine lurched sideways one time too many. Amy watched the canoe follow the momentum dumping passengers, rods and tackle. She breathed a sigh of relief when three heads broke the surface of the water.

"Swim to the canoe, Elaine," Henry called.

There was no need for concern here; she could handle herself in the water. While Henry and Ted rescued floating cushions and paddles, their passenger took a few strokes and clung to the side of the vessel.

Amy's eyes centered on Ted. She expected to see a cloud of blue smoke rise above his red hair and hear a string of cuss words known only to sailors. But he kept his composure, climbed up on the capsized craft, straddled it, and began to paddle toward shore with Henry and Elaine in tow.

Rummaging through a sack, Amy found the matches, struck a flame and ignited the wood already prepared for a fire. In no time, a radiant heat welcomed the water-logged swimmers.

"Take your shoes off and set them on these rocks by the fire, Elaine," Amy instructed. "And go change. The tent is all yours."

Henry and Ted grabbed their backpacks and headed into the woods. They returned to the fire clad in dry clothes wringing out jeans, shirts and socks.

"Hey, Henry, look in that tool bag of mine," said Ted. "I brought some spare rope. We need to string us a line to dry our things on."

"Sounds like a plan. How 'bout between those two birches?"

By the time the men had a clothesline in place, Elaine emerged from the tent. Her demeanor was humble, the curl in her hair hung in limp threads, and mascara ran under her eyes. She sniffled and started to sneeze.

"Hang your things on that rope and come over and let the fire warm you up. We don't want you to get chilled," Henry directed. "We'll have some coffee going here shortly. I'll get the Coleman lit."

Amy looked at Ted and teased, "My, Ted, how clever of you to think of hanging a clothesline out here in the middle of nowhere. Who'd a guessed we'd be needing one."

"Say no more, little lady, or you'll be looking for a spot to hang your shirt and pants!"

"Got your message," she came back with a grin.

Before long, the coffee was perking in a white enamel pot while the stew bubbled in the cast iron skillet. Paper plates served as dinner china. Four hungry souls devoured a loaf of Thelma's fresh bread until nothing was left but the end crust. It was a simple but satisfying meal.

Afterward, Elaine made a confession. "I suppose it was my fault you lost your fish, Ted."

"Not to mention the tackle box," he volunteered.

"I apologize, guys. You've both been such good sports about it."

"Think of it as an experience to tell your grandchildren, Elaine," replied Henry. "It's not the first time Ted or me have been dumped out of a canoe."

"Tell my grandchildren!" Elaine's voice rose an octave. "I can't get that daughter of mine to settle for one man long enough to get married. I must say, though, Matt's caught her eye."

Amy choked on her coffee. Ted looked at her and grinned.

"I hear a boat coming in now," said Henry. "Knew Matt would stay out 'til almost dark. He's one determined fisherman."

"Bet they're starving!" Amy reached for the container with the stew and dumped it into the skillet. Thank goodness Thelma sent plenty of bread."

The sound of snapping branches and pine needles grew louder as Lyle emerged from the shadows, "Matt and Sonja are securing the boat."

"Any luck?" asked Henry.

"Just a few small bass. We threw 'em back. There's gotta be some lunkers hiding under those weed beds, though. Always tomorrow. Right now, I could use a cup of hot coffee."

"There's one cup left with your name on it, Lyle," Amy said as she offered it to him. "I'll go get more water and brew another pot."

As Amy made her way toward the lake in the lingering light, she saw the shadows of two people form a silhouette against the darkening water. She stopped short as their bodies molded into one. Her legs turned to stone and her heart sank. She was trapped. Intrusion was out of the question, yet, she couldn't return to the others without water. Feeling powerless, her eyes transfixed on the darkening images before her, Amy heard Matt's voice as he removed the arms that encircled his neck.

"Whoa, Sonja, you've got the wrong impression! You're a lot of fun, but that's as far as it goes." Matt put some distance between them.

Sonja's arms stiffened and her hands balled into fists. She threw out her chest and cocked her head to one side allowing her hair to fall across pouting lips, "I can't believe you would turn me down, Matt. I've never had a man do that! Admit it—-you think I'm hot. I know you do"

"No argument there."

"Then what's wrong? Gay?"

Matt's laughter echoed across the still water. "Not that I've noticed. Nor, I might add, have any of my female dates."

Sonja stomped her foot and gave it one last shot. "There has to be a reason. Men find me irresistible. Why don't you?"

"I have my reasons, Sonja."

"And I bet she's at home waiting for you."

"Let's just drop it, all right?"

As Matt and Sonja walked down the shoreline their conversation faded into the night.

With a heavy heart, Amy realized this chance encounter shed new light on her attraction to Matt. She heard him admit to Sonja that he dated other women. Why shouldn't he? He was eligible. But in the back of her mind was a nagging thought. Had he assumed that night on the beach that she was a naïve country girl eager for a stranger's attention? Amy wiped at humiliating tears that blurred her vision and she stumbled to the edge of the lake. Splashing handfuls of cool liquid onto her face cleared her eyes but the more she thought about any relationship with Matt, the more confused she became. Try as she might, she couldn't forget his kiss.

Then, taking a big breath, she regained her composure, filled the water can, and started toward the campfire.

Back at the site while everyone was talking about the incident with the canoe, Amy replenished the coffee. Ted admitted, "I've lost a few big ones in my day, but never like that!"

Amy took notice that Sonja was not sitting near Matt but had wedged herself between Ted and Elaine. Amy sat back in her lawn chair and observed. Sonja, as Amy saw it, was like a black widow spider setting up her male for the inevitable sting, but she knew Ted was nobody's fool; he'd play the game, but he'd seen the light.

"Ted, you've got to take me out in the canoe tomorrow," Sonja pleaded. "I promise to behave myself."

"It seems to me, I've heard that one before. One of you Newman ladies is enough for me."

"I'm a good pupil, and I know you'd be an excellent teacher." Slim fingers inched their way up the side of Ted's arm and pinched his cheek. "What do you say?"

"Why don't we sleep on it?"

"Speaking of sleep," Lyle interrupted, "I'm ready to call it a day. Where do you want us to bed down, Henry?"

"The girls can have the tent. Holds three."

Amy was quick to respond. "Take my place, Lyle. I like the open spaces."

"Well, I won't fight you on that one," Lyle commented.

Amy grabbed her sleeping bag, and headed toward the water, tossing over her shoulder, "The lapping waves lull me to sleep."

She hoped they bought that! She needed to be alone, away from giggling women, and with distance between her and Matt.

Amy selected a grassy spot near the water, climbed into the sleeping bag, and on her back, she surveyed the night sky. A scattering of stars twinkled overhead and every now and then a gust of wind swept around her, sending shivers through her body. She regretted giving up her place in the tent, but she was stuck with her decision.

Sometime during the night, Amy woke to feel raindrops falling on her face. The wind was getting stronger and in the distance thunder rumbled. Amy gave a long sigh. The last thing they needed tonight was an electrical storm. In a matter of seconds, lightening skipped across the sky, illuminating the water below. Another boom of thunder gave fair warning that Mother Nature meant business. That was enough for Amy. She knew it was too close for comfort and she needed to get back with the others.

She pulled her body into a sitting position, but like a moth caught in a cocoon, she was unable to free herself. She had pulled the zipper up to her neck and her arms were pined against her sides. The smallest opening allowed her fingers to wiggle out to grasp the tab of the zipper. At first the metal teeth opened but a sudden boom of thunder unnerved Amy and she pulled down too fast snagging the material. She pulled and tugged, but to no avail. It was stuck! Another flash of lightening lit up the sky heightening her determination. Blood rushed to her heart and her pulse quickened. Breath came in shallow pants as fear bordered on panic. Feeling a surge of strength, she gave one last yank before calling for help. A sudden ripping sound opened the metal track and her arms sprang free. She flung the sleeping bag away from her body.

No sooner was she on her feet when the wind swept across the lake knocking her down again. This time she heard the splitting of wood and then a huge thump.

"Help!" Her scream rode away with the wind.

Less than twenty feet away a solitary pine tree crashed to the ground. The tree, once standing straight as a sentinel, now lay as a barrier between Amy and the others. In the darkness everything looked the same. Her eyes strained to see something familiar. Suddenly, they saw a flicker of light and she heard Matt's voice, "Amy, over here. To your right. Follow the light."

Groping toward the lantern, she felt the wind whipping her hair into a frenzy and pellets of rain stinging her face. At last she stood before Matt. She could not control her shaking. Every fiber vibrated and without a moment's thought, she reached out to him and buried her face in his chest. Comforting arms gathered her close.

By this time, Henry and Ted were shouting, "Amy! Amy!" "It's all right, Henry, she's with me." Matt tightened his hold.

"For an independent gal, you have a way of getting yourself in some tight spots, don't you?"

"Seems that way," Amy said turning her face upward.

"I should have watched you more carefully."

"Watched me? I don't understand."

"I couldn't sleep so I've been sitting looking out over the lake. I saw the storm coming, but had no idea the wind would hit so hard." His voice softened but he reprimanded, "You shouldn't been down there alone."

One hand gently touched the side of Amy's face and she knew he was going to kiss her. Earlier, her pride might have stopped him, but right now, in her shaken condition, the moment was hers and she loved him too much to resist. With each breath, her temperature rose and her body, already limp from fear, clung to him for support. Tender, moist lips pressed against hers, suctioning the breath out of her while massaging fingers played with the nape of her neck. Finally, Matt whispered against her cheek, "Amy I..."

His words hung in the air as another violent gust of wind blew in the tent and Sonja and Elaine's screams shattered the moment.

"Matt, bring your light!" Ted shouted.

Everyone rushed to the ill-fated tent and two ill-tempered campers.

"Father, if you ever suggest camping again...!"

"How'd I know it'd blow up a storm. Looked fine when we turned in."

"It's a freak storm," Henry consoled. "They come up out of nowhere. No point in trying to put the tent back up. It'll never hold in this wind."

"Bring the sleeping bags in under these spruce branches," Ted said. "Stay close together, too, for warmth."

"Mine's down by the shore if the wind hasn't blown it in the lake."

"We can share." Matt responded, "If that's all right with you."

There was more wind than rain. Still, sleep was impossible. A sorry-looking group of campers met the dawn. From the tossing and turning and the moans and groans heard throughout the night, it was evident no one had slept.

Henry was the first to rise. "I'll have the coffee ready in a jiff, folks. Warm you right up. Amy how 'bout frying some bacon and eggs?"

"Just what we need, Daddy." She jumped up from Matt's sleeping bag and went to retrieve food from the cooler.

"To think I could still be asleep at the cabin," yawned Sonja.

"And miss the best part of the day!" Ted teased. "When's the last time you saw a sunrise, Sonja?"

She ran her fingers slowly through tussled blond hair and batted her eyelids at him. "Well..., if you really want to know it was a couple months ago. Of course, I was just getting home from a date. Does that count?"

Ted shook his head from side to side. "Somethin' tells me a sunrise was the last thing on your mind."

"O.K., O.K. So where's this dazzling dawn? Looks like nothin' but gray mist out there to me."

"Like they say, 'beauty is in the eye of the beholder.'"

"Well, my eyes are tired and the only thing I'd like to behold right now is a hot cup of coffee."

The gas from the Coleman burner burst into yellow and blue flame as one by one bubbles of perked coffee threatened to overflow the spout.

Amy hoped that a good, hot breakfast would put everyone in better spirits. The eggs were almost cooked when a sudden cloudburst soaked the skillet, the paper plates, and the rest of Thelma's bread.

"This is the last straw!" Sonja complained. "Let's go home."

"I'll second that," piped up her mother.

The two women met no opposition. The weather didn't look promising and fishing in the rain was out of the question, so all agreed to return to the lodge. This time there were no rest stops along the way.

Amy knew the sound of the motors would stir Thelma's curiosity since she didn't expect to see them until evening. Sure enough, as they approached the dock, she was standing on the porch scrutinizing the boats with Lawrence painted on the side. After docking, two of the women took off running and left the others to unload the equipment.

Amy appeared on the porch steps several minutes later with a backpack slung over each shoulder and a box of cooking utensils in her arms.

Thelma rushed out to relieve some of her load. "Good gracious, girl, you look a sight! What's goin' on? Why're you home? Thought this was s'possed to be a big deal?"

"Oh, it was a big deal all right! Complaining, whiny

women, an upset canoe, no sleep and to top it off, I came close to getting hit by a tree in the storm last night!"

"Amy Lawrence! I told you not to go. And what about breakfast? Did you cook anything?"

"Started to but we got washed out."

"Well, I'll have the bacon frying and the eggs scrambled in no time. Spread the word." Thelma started back into the kitchen but Amy stopped her.

"Don't bother, Thelma. My guess is that everyone's heading for bed. I know I am. It was a rough night! At least most of it was."

"You mean there was a bright spot?"

A faint smile brightened Amy's weary face. "Too tired to tell you. You'll have to wait."

Without another word, Amy climbed the stairs to her room. The memory of Matt's second kiss lingered on her lips.

Chapter Twenty-two

For the better part of the day, there was little activity around the lodge. Everyone, except Thelma, caught up on lost sleep. By two o'clock, the rain stopped and the clouds pulled back their gray curtain to expose a sliver of sunlight. Gradually, the sky brightened until only a small bank of clouds slipped into the west.

It was close to four in the afternoon when Amy, awakened by the clanging and banging of pots and pans, walked down to the kitchen to see what all the commotion was about. Her eyes surveyed freshly baked bread and peach pies on the cupboard, fresh vegetables in the sink waiting to be scrubbed, and a huge golden-brown turkey roasting in the oven.

"Thelma, what's all this? Turkey? We must have gotten some unexpected guests while I was gone."

"Nobody new, but yes, we're having company for supper. Your father invited Matt and the Newmans to eat with us tonight. Feels bad that things didn't work out."

"It was unreal, Thelma. I wish you could've been there when the tent collapsed!"

Thelma shook with laughter. "Your father told me about that little problem. I'm sure it wasn't amusing to Elaine and Sonja, but I can imagine those two crawling out from under that mess!"

"Something tells me the next time Lyle is struck by the 'call of the wild', he'll be going alone."

"So the trip was a total disaster from beginning to end, eh?"

"Well," Amy hesitated, "I wouldn't say it was all a disaster."

"Oh, you mean there were some high spots? Spill the beans, little lady."

"I overheard a conversation between Matt and Sonja."

Thelma put the last potato she was peeling in the pot, wiped her hands on her apron, and gave her full attention to Amy. "Oh, yeah?"

"He told her plain and simple he's not interested. At least not the way she'd like him to be."

"How'd she take that?"

"Not well. She insisted on a reason. Told him he's the first to turn her down."

"Probably true but what did he tell her?"

"Said he had his reasons and suggested they drop it."

"Yes!" Thelma gave the thumbs up sign. "He is my kind of man!"

* * *

By six o'clock, Thelma was pacing the floor waiting for everyone to come eat. She'd arranged the center-piece on the dining room table three times in the last half hour. Finally, she decided the clear glass bowl with the floating water lilies looked best on the pale blue tablecloth.

It wasn't long before Amy arrived in the kitchen looking fresh and renewed from her camping ordeal. An ankle length dress swayed against tanned legs and its soft shade of yellow complimented the tinge of pink in her cheeks. Shining, auburn hair bounced around her delicate neck as she tried to fasten the back zipper.

"Thelma, please zip me up."

"My, my, aren't we going all out tonight!"

"If you can serve a special dinner, then the least I can do is dress for it."

"You're sure it's me you want to impress?"

"Now that you mention it, there might be another party involved."

"I knew it. All I can say is if a certain fellow in cabin eight isn't impressed, then there's something wrong with that guy."

The sound of footsteps on the porch put an end to their conversation. The Newmans arrived, Lyle exclaiming, "Is that turkey I smell. Hallelujah! My favorite!"

Amy's eyes widened at the transformation in Elaine and Sonja. There was no comparison to the two distraught and haggard looking females seen earlier. A few hours sleep, freshly shampooed hair, and fresh make-up did magic. Sonja's blond hair was pulled back from her face and hung in a braid accenting her high cheek bones and wide-set blue eyes.

"Thelma," she said, "you wouldn't believe what we've had to eat the last twenty-four hours! I can't wait to eat some real food."

"Oh, I thought Amy was a pretty fair cook."

"My dear," Elaine cut in, "I'm sure Sonja didn't mean to imply it was Amy's fault. It's just that campfire cooking can't be compared to anything you prepare. And then breakfast was completely rained out!"

"Rest assured, I made plenty. It'll be your own fault if you go hungry tonight. I even baked Ted's favorite peach pie, but Henry says not to count on his coming."

Sonja's jaw dropped and she was quick to question, "You mean Ted won't be here for dinner?"

Amy enlightened her. "He has to catch up on some work he missed yesterday. Business sometimes has to come first, you know."

"Well, that's plain ridiculous! He can't do that to me." Sonja's irritation was mounting. "I told him we'd be leaving in a day or so. Thought he wanted to spend more time with me."

"Ted's full of surprises, Sonja." Amy commented.

"You know dear," Elaine tried to calm her daughter, "Some people do have to work for a living."

"I'm sure he isn't doing anything that can't wait for tomorrow. What's his number? You don't mind if I call him, do you, Thelma?"

"Fine with me. His number's written on that list above the phone."

"Sonja, why are you so determined to see Ted this evening?" Elaine asked. "What happened to Matt?"

Sonja's eyes bore into her mother's. "Mo-th-er, I explained things to you at the cottage—remember?"

"Oh, I'm sorry, dear. Now I do recall our conversation but you know I was half asleep."

Waving her mother aside, Sonja reached for the phone, dialed Ted's number and turned on the charm.

"Ted, it's Sonja. You are coming for dinner, aren't you? I really want to see you again before we leave and besides, Thelma baked your favorite peach pie. She insists that you come." A short pause passed before she began again. "Another half hour isn't going to hurt. We'll wait for you. See you, Ted."

As she hung up the phone she flashed a triumphant smile. "He'll be here in thirty minutes."

Chapter Twenty-three

Two raps on the back door caught Amy's attention. She opened it to find Matt looking rested and clean-shaven, dressed in a white Izod shirt and a pair of blue Levis. For a moment he looked at her without speaking. Amy broke the silence.

"Hi there. I see you've recovered. C'mon in."

"Sorry I'm late. Overslept."

"No, no. We're waiting on Ted."

Matt acknowledged the other women and then excused himself to find Henry and Lyle by the fireplace.

As Amy walked into the dining room to set a place for Ted, Sonja followed and cornered her by the table. Lowering her voice she began, "If you'd like a piece of advice, Amy, I wouldn't waste my time on Matt."

The plate Amy was carrying almost slipped from her hand as she turned to face Sonja. "I beg your pardon. What are you talking about?"

"You know what I mean. I saw how you cozied up to

him last night. Telling everyone your sleeping bag was blown in the lake."

"He offered to share his. Get your facts straight."

"Oh, I'll tell you some facts, Honey. Matt told me himself he's in love with a girl back home. Probably going to marry her this fall. This fishing trip was sort of a last fling-- guy thing. From one girl to another, Amy, I wouldn't want to see you make a fool of yourself."

The nauseating smugness Amy saw in Sonja's eyes made her blood boil but she refused to take the bait. She would admit nothing to this blond bimbo even if her biting words were true.

"You tend to your business, Sonja, and I'll tend to mine. Now why don't you get out of my way while I help Thelma get this meal on the table."

The sound of Ted's approaching boat sent Sonja running out the door to meet him.

"Now that Ted's here, we can dish up the food, Amy. Sure didn't think he'd give in to her whining. Guess she's got his number, though."

"Don't count on it. Ted told me he's figured her out. He's just playing the game. Truth is—-your cooking won him over."

"Well, now, as I recall, the man does like to eat."

By the time Ted and Sonja walked in, the dining room table was covered with bowls of steaming vegetables, stuffing, gravy and rolls. In the center, on a huge white platter, was Thelma's specialty—-a golden-skinned turkey. The aroma alone brought everyone from the living room to gather round the table. Sonja seated herself between Matt and Ted. Amy sat opposite, beside Elaine and Lyle. Henry and Thelma took their places at each end.

Everyone joined hands as Henry offered a blessing. He wasted no time in carving the turkey until not much was left but the skeleton.

"Great carcass for a pot of soup," observed Elaine. "I

think I know what's going to be on the menu this week. Right, Thelma?"

"No question about it. I'll see that you're the first to taste it, Elaine."

"I'm afraid we may not be around," said Lyle.

"Oh?" Henry quizzed. "Thinking of going home?"

"Been gone longer than I intended. Can't be away from the office too long." He chuckled as he continued, "They'll think they can run it without me."

Elaine piped up, "It was a lucky break for us, though, that we found the lodge, especially since Lyle tells me you won't be operating it next summer."

"For heavens sake, why not, Henry?" Sonja asked.

"New folks are buying the place."

"Well, won't they carry on as usual?"

"Mining companies don't operate fishing lodges," Amy commented.

"You mean a mining company is buying Pine Lake Lodge? I can't believe you'd do that! How terrible!"

"Sometimes circumstances force us to do things we don't want to do, Sonja."

"Well, then, Father," her voice grew louder, "why don't you buy it? A summer home. With all these cottages, we could invite our friends and you could entertain clients with the fishing."

Amy's eyes glared at Sonja in disbelief! She'd rather see Canadian Uranium buy the lodge than have this girl take her place. Ted was quick to step in, "Aw, c'mon now Sonja, you'd be bored stiff in a week. No fancy parties, no big shops, and not much night life."

"But Ted," her voice softened and she slipped a hand around his reddening neck, "you'd be around to keep my life interesting."

The ringing of the telephone ended the conversation and Henry walked into the kitchen to answer it. In a few seconds, he called out, "It's for you, Matt. Lady by the name of Barbara Anderson."

"Great! I've been waiting to hear from her." Matt got up from the table and headed toward the kitchen.

"Take it in my office, Matt. More privacy."

"Thanks, I will." Three pairs of curious eyes followed him out of the room.

Matt returned to find everyone savoring peach pie and drinking coffee. In fact, Ted was on his second piece.

"How are things at home, Matt?" Sonja arched her eyebrows.

"Just fine. Couldn't be better."

"When are you leaving? Elaine asked.

Amy tried not to look interested as she poured herself another cup of coffee but she didn't miss a word.

"Probably in a day or so. Got to get home to see some folks. Got some things to attend to."

Amy lowered her eyes. She couldn't look at him, not after seeing his eager reaction to the phone call. She didn't want to admit it, but maybe Sonja was right after all.

There was no denying the intentional kick to Amy's foot under the table and the expression on her face that clearly meant, 'told you so.'

Amy had heard enough. She excused herself and went to the kitchen. From the pile of dirty dishes stacked on the cupboard she knew she'd be busy for the next hour or so. She hoped the activity would keep her mind off her churning stomach. She was elbow deep in soap suds when Ted and Sonja walked over to her.

"I'd help you clean up, Amy, but Ted and I are going into town for some excitement."

"Excitement?" Amy asked, looking at Ted.

"There's a dance at the town hall. We might take in a pint at the pub, too."

"Are you sure you can handle all that in one night, Sonja?"

"Don't you worry your little head 'bout what I can

118

handle, Honey. Are you ready, Ted?"

Thelma walked into the kitchen as Sonja was ushering Ted out the door. "Where on earth are you two off to?"

"Thought I'd show Sonja some nightlife," grinned Ted.

"I'm surprised you can walk at all after what you packed away at dinner," teased Thelma. "You be careful in that boat—'specially after dark."

"No problem. I swear by now I could do it with my eyes closed. Thanks again for supper."

"Behave yourself, Ted," Amy called as they walked down the steps.

"Not if I have anything to do with it," Sonja laughed slipping her hand into Ted's.

Thelma sighed and shook her head. "That man has his hands full tonight."

Chapter Twenty-four

Twilight turned into darkness by the time Amy put the last cup and saucer on the shelf. Lyle and Elaine left earlier, Thelma was upstairs writing letters, and Matt and Henry were in his office. Amy sought solitude so she walked out to the front porch and stood listening to the symphony of crickets and frogs. There was no need for pretense here. Salty tears erupted from her eyes meandering over her cheekbones until they dripped off her chin. She'd been a fool to believe Matt cared for her. It was almost a relief to know he'd soon be leaving. Out of sight; out of mind.

The screeching of the screen door interrupted her train of thought. Amy turned her head just enough to see Matt close it, then she faced the lake again. The delicate scent of his after shave reached her before he did.

"I thought you might be out here. Hoped you would be. Amy, I have to talk to you." She felt the warmth of his hands as he stood behind her gently squeezing her shoulders.

Here it comes-the big confession!

Not having the courage to face him, and with a trembling voice she said, "No explanations, please. Spare me. And don't touch me."

"Amy, what's wrong? What did I do?" He swung round to face her.

"I actually believed you were beginning to care about me. The night on the beach? The camping trip?"

"Amy, I do care. I'm in love with you." One hand tilted her chin upward as he bent to kiss her. His lips grazed the surface of hers when she turned her head away. There was no giving in this time.

"Matt, do you expect me to believe that? Sorry to disappoint you, but I'm not the naïve, backwoods girl you apparently think I am. Sweet talk won't cut it! I'm not a vacation fling, Matt! Never have been, and never will be! Isn't one woman enough for you?"

"I've never thought of you as naïve, Amy, and I certainly never thought of you as a vacation fling! And as far as another woman is concerned, I don't know what you mean."

"Then I suggest you and Sonja get your stories straight."

With that, Amy yanked Matt's hand from her arm and ran toward the door. The last words she heard were, "Sonja? What? Wait a minute! Amy, please listen…"

Once upstairs, Amy fell across the bed and buried her head in her pillow. Again the tears flowed. To hear Matt say that he loved her now was like throwing salt on her wounded heart. Emotionally drained, she unzipped the dress threw it in a heap on the floor, and slipped under the sheets. Sleep did not come. Unlike Henry, whose deep nasal snore drifted down the hall to break the silence, she couldn't relax. A glance at her clock showed it was a few minutes past three. Would this night never end?

An unfamiliar noise aroused her curiosity. She sat up

in bed and listened. Rap, rap, rap. It sounded as though someone was knocking at the back door. Slipping on a robe, she started down the stairs. The raps grew more urgent! Amy wondered why anyone would disturb them at this hour? In her haste, she tripped on the bottom of her robe and as she reached out to steady herself, she saw the silhouette of a man against the dim light of the moon. She turned on the porch light and to her surprise saw Lyle. He held up his hand to knock again when she opened the door.

"Lyle, is something wrong?"

"Sorry, Amy, but Sonja isn't home yet. We're worried sick! I thought I could trust Ted. They have to make that trip in the dark! Never should have let her go."

By this time, Henry heard the commotion and was on his way to the kitchen. Looking bewildered, wearing only jeans, and with white shocks of hair sticking out at odd angles from his circular fringe, he asked, "Kyle, someone sick?"

"No, Ted and Sonja haven't come home. Elaine is beside herself and I'm not too thrilled either. What do you suppose has happened?"

"Probably just lost track of time. Young folks."

"Oh, my daughter's a night owl all right. Wouldn't be the first time but I'm worried about the trip on the lake."

Henry tried to reassure a worried father. "Ted knows this lake as well as I do but I understand your concern. Just give me a minute to dress and I'll ride up the lake to see if there's any sign of them."

"Let me go with you, Daddy. I haven't been sleeping anyway." Amy tried not to show alarm but she felt something was amiss. She knew Ted well enough to know he wouldn't intentionally worry Sonja's parents. Besides, if they did go to the pub, by law it had to close at two a.m.

"I can't tell you how much I appreciate this, Henry. Elaine will be so relieved. But Amy, Sonja's my concern; you needn't go."

"Don't mind in the least. Stay with Elaine. She'll feel better with you."

"All right, you have a point. She's upset."

Thelma's light was on when Amy went back upstairs to change clothes.

"Amy, did I hear voices in the kitchen or was I dreaming?"

"It was Lyle. Ted and Sonja aren't back yet."

"They really did intend to make a night of it, didn't they?"

"I have a suspicion Ted may have bitten off more than he can chew."

"You may be right, but there's a possibility he had motor trouble."

"That I know he can handle. His company may be another matter."

"Lyle isn't going out looking for them, is he?"

"No, Daddy and I are going to ride up to the marina."

"Dress warmly, Amy. This night air'll chill you to the bone."

Amy knew enough to heed Thelma's advice. She pulled on a pair of jeans, a sweater, and a jacket. Just thinking about the damp air sent shivers up her spine.

The motor was purring and Henry was untying the rope when Amy stepped on the dock. She saw someone else in the boat, too. Surmising that Lyle must have changed his mind, Amy turned on her flashlight, stepped over the side, and looked, not into Lyle's face, but Matt's.

The darkness hid her look of astonishment, but her words gave her away, "What are you doing here?"

"The same thing you are. Sit down. Your father doesn't have time to waste."

Ignoring his commanding tone, Amy shouted over the noise of the motor, "What's the best way to help, Daddy?"

"Matt has a strong light, too, so you shine yours on one side and let him handle the other. I'll stop the motor every now and then and call Ted's name. He may have sheared a cotter pin and is floating off shore somewhere."

"We sure didn't need this fog rolling in. It's hard enough to see in the dark."

"I'll take it slow."

The further they went, the more Amy's eyes played tricks on her. Grotesque, twisted shapes turned out to be no more than a sagging tree or a water-logged stump. Henry's call was answered by his own echo. The missing couple was nowhere to be seen.

After the fourth stop, Amy offered her opinion. "I have a hunch they're not on the lake at all. Sonja was determined Ted would show her a good time before she left. Time means nothing to her."

"Amy may have a point, Henry," Matt said. "Why don't we head on down to the marina and see if the boat's there. If not, we can continue the search from that end."

"Anything's worth a try," Henry agreed. "Let's hope it's there."

The dampness sent shivers racing through Amy and shook her whole body. Henry took notice and said, "Sit with Matt. He can shield you from the wind. No need in you catching pneumonia because of this wild goose chase!"

Amy protested, "Really, I'm fine." Her chattering teeth told the truth.

"Your father knows best, young lady." Matt reached over, caught her arm, and had her half way out of the seat when Henry turned the motor full throttle. The boat sped forward and Amy went with it. She ended up on Matt's lap with his arms pulling her close to him.

"This is not what my father had in mind, and you know it!" She struggled to get free but Matt was equally determined. "Like it or not, Henry's right. So just relax."

There was no use fighting him. She leaned back and let her head fall against Matt's chest. For the first time in her life she understood the dichotomy between pleasure and pain. His nearness still thrilled her but she knew he was not hers to keep.

They traveled a mile when Henry called, "I see lights from the marina. Shine your light over to the left, Matt. We should be able to make out the dock soon."

Matt promptly reached around Amy and picked up his Coleman. The bright beam bounced off the side of Ted's boat tied to a ring in the planking.

"That's one welcome sight!" Henry exclaimed.

"Ted's car is parked under that night light so they must be upstairs in his apartment," observed Amy.

It wasn't long before a door slammed and footsteps started running down the steps and toward the pier. Ted showed no surprise when he saw the boat's occupants.

"Don't tell me. I know why you're here."

"Ted, at three- thirty in the morning, this is hardly a social call," Amy reminded him.

"I'm sorry. Let me explain. I should've brought her home sooner, but we were at the pub and we ran into some friends I hadn't seen in a while. You know how that goes. Before I realized it, they were closing the place. Sonja was having a great time——didn't want to leave."

Matt and Henry joined in the conversation with a simultaneous, "Well, where is she now?"

Ted cleared his throat and paused a moment before answering, "That's the problem."

"You mean she's not here!" Amy cried.

"Oh, she's here——stretched out on the bed upstairs."

Matt started to laugh, Henry shook his head, and Amy's mouth flew open.

Ted suddenly explained, "Oh, no, you don't understand. She's passed out. Guess she had one drink too many! Several actually. That's why I couldn't bring her home. Can you imagine Lyle's reaction?"

"That's why we're here, Ted. Both Elaine and Lyle were worried you'd run into trouble with the boat."

126

"That kind of trouble I can handle," sighed Ted. "What am I going to do with her? She can't go home in that condition."

"I guess you're stuck with her until she sleeps it off, buddy." Matt gave Ted a good-natured slap on the back.

"Listen, my brother comes back in the morning. I'd never hear the end of it. Besides her parents..." Ted threw up his hands in exasperation. "I should've known she was trouble the first time I saw her."

"Amen!" added Amy.

As usual, Henry had the solution. "There's only one thing to do. Probably for the first time in her life, Sonja's going to have to face the music. We'll take her back just the way she is. I'm sure Lyle will have a few choice words for her when she wakes up."

"Lyle won't be the only one," Matt interjected. "I have some she won't forget either."

Oh, really? Amy thought. That's interesting.

"Let's get the sleeping beauty," Henry said. "I've got a business appointment at ten, and so far, it's been a short night."

Ted didn't waste a moment carrying Sonja out of his apartment and into the waiting boat. As he placed her limp body on the cushions, Amy noticed Sonja's outfit was nothing but light-weight cotton.

"She's going to 'catch her death' in those Capri's and skimpy shirt."

"Here," Matt said, taking off his jacket, "put this around her."

"Matt, you'll freeze!" The words slipped out of Amy's mouth before she realized it.

"Do I detect a hint of concern? Like you'd care?"

The old sarcasm was back so she ignored his remark while Ted solved the problem. "I'll get a blanket."

As he tucked it around Sonja, she mumbled something inaudible, but there was no doubt she was oblivious to the commotion she'd caused.

The earlier fog had lifted and Henry was able to pilot the boat with more speed in the open water. Before long, a flicker of light a short distance ahead beckoned them home. As they approached the main dock, Amy saw Lyle pacing back and forth. As he reached out to catch the bow of the boat, his eyes focused on his daughter lying on the bottom.

"Sonja! Henry what happened? Is she all right?"

"She's fine—doesn't hold her drinks too well, though."

"You mean she and Ted were out in his boat at this hour in this condition? Wait 'til I get my hands on that young…"

"Calm down, Lyle." said Henry. "First of all, Ted is sober and he had more sense than to try and bring her home alone in his boat. They were at the marina. Ted feels terrible but I don't think he should be held responsible for your daughter's drinking habits." The long night had given Henry a short fuse.

"I'm sorry. You're right. This isn't the first time Sonja has had too much to drink. We've seen her brought home in this condition more than once."

Elaine came running down the dock calling, "Lyle? Where's Sonja?"

"Come see for yourself. As usual, had too many and passed out."

"Oh, no! She promised it wouldn't happen again. You've every right to be upset with us, Henry. Sending you out in the middle of the night is bad enough."

"We won't worry about a little lost sleep, Elaine. Amy hold the boat steady while Matt and I lift her out."

Sonja made a few moans as she was picked up, but her eyes remained closed.

"Let me carry her, Matt," Lyle insisted. You've done enough already."

"She's dead weight. Better if we both carry her."

"I'll bring the lantern," offered Amy.

She walked ahead and let the beam of light fall behind her making it easier for Matt to follow. The men got Sonja up the steps, into the cottage, and placed on the bed.

"You can handle her from here, Elaine. By the way, I'd like a word with her in the morning. O.K.?"

"Sure thing. Thanks Matt."

Amy expected Matt to turn and go on to his own cabin once they reached the bottom of the porch steps, but instead, he hesitated, then said, "Amy, can we talk?"

"Talking won't change the facts, Matt. I heard all I needed to hear. It's almost morning; get some sleep."

The darkness took her away.

Chapter Twenty-five

"What a fantastic day, folks! Makes you happy to be alive. Get out there and make the most of it!" The voice of some radio disc jockey drifted up the stairs and tickled Amy's ears until one leaden eye opened after the other. A quick glance at the clock told her she'd gotten a mere four hours sleep. Searching for Sonja and Ted until almost dawn was not her idea of a good time.

As Amy let the cool spray from the shower pulsate against her weary body, she thought about last night. One phone call had decimated her hope of a truthful relationship with Matt. How could she ever forget the name Barbara Anderson?

"Thelma," Amy said as she poured herself a cup of coffee, "You have no idea how much I need every ounce of caffeine in this mug today."

"If the circles under your eyes are any clue, then drink up, girl. Your father didn't have much time to give me the whole story but I gather things got interesting last night."

"To say the least. Speaking of Daddy, where is he?"

"Went to town to meet that mining company fellow. He looked beat—only had a few hours sleep. Today is the day, remember?"

"Don't remind me. With everything else these past couple days, I completely forgot."

"How much do you suppose Sonja remembers this morning?"

"My guess is very little. She must have cleaned out the pub! Sure was in sorry condition. According to Lyle, this is not uncommon."

"Not surprised."

"She's lucky she had Ted looking out for her." Amy chuckled, "But he was walking on coals—didn't know what he was going to do with her. Thought she'd have to spend the night with him."

"And Ted didn't like the idea?"

"Believe it or not, he was really concerned folks would get the wrong impression. Ted likes his fun, Thelma, but he's a decent guy at heart."

"Oh, I've always known that. It's just that someone like Sonja must be a big temptation. But then, Matt didn't give in to her, did he?"

"She's not his type, I guess." Amy took another sip of coffee. She didn't care for the direction this conversation was taking.

"I have a feeling I know his kind."

"And how do you know that?"

"He didn't take his eyes off you all evening, Amy. Some things a person can sense. He cares for you; mark my words. And I think you know it, too. Why are you holding back? It's what you want, isn't it?"

"Please, Thelma." Amy walked over to the sink and deposited her cup in some hot sudsy water. "I don't want to talk about it. What's the point in deluding myself? We both know there's someone else in his life. You saw how eager he was to talk to that woman on the phone last night. He came right out and said he had to return to the states for a personal commitment."

Thelma was not ready to give up. "You've heard, from an unreliable source, that Matt has a fiancé, but that doesn't make it a fact."

"Thelma, I heard the phone. Daddy called out her name, and I saw the anticipation on Matt's face when he went for the call. Those are cold, hard facts."

"It's your life, honey. I'm telling you the way I see it."

"Thelma, I've always valued your opinion, but this time I have to work it out by myself. I've got to be sure. The hurt from Eric still haunts me. Anyway, in a day or so he'll be gone and with Daddy signing the final papers on the lodge today, I'm going to be too busy packing to give Matt much thought."

"I don't believe a word of it. It's going to take more than a few weeks of busy work to erase that man's memory, and you know it!"

The sound of approaching voices ended their discussion. Amy turned and looked out the window to see Lyle, Elaine, and Sonja climbing the steps to the back porch. She opened the door with a cheery, "Good morning!"

"Amy, do you have to yell?" Sonja asked. "My head is splitting."

"Through no fault but your own," Lyle reminded her.

"Please, Father, I've had enough badgering about my behavior to last an eternity. Bad enough hearing it from you, but I didn't expect to get a lecture from Matt, too. I promised I'd tell Amy I'm sorry for all the disruption."

Amy heard no remorse and there was no actual apology. Stepping into the kitchen, Elaine explained, "This isn't a social call. We're leaving today and we need to settle our account with you."

Trying to sound cordial, Thelma said, "I hope you've

enjoyed your stay with us."

Elaine's smile appeared genuine. "It's been grand. Such a shame the lodge is going to be sold. I understand Henry is with the buyer now. We told him last night we'd be leaving and he explained that he had an early appointment."

"Come into the office," Amy instructed.

"You go, Father." Sonja reached into the cupboard for a mug. I'm dying for a cup of Thelma's coffee. Black, please."

Elaine and Lyle followed Amy while Sonja sank down into a chair and leaned her head in her hands. She removed stylish sunglasses that had concealed her blood-shot eyes.

"I was a naughty girl last night, Thelma. If it's any comfort to all concerned, I'm paying for it today."

"So are the rest of us. We usually get a little more than four hours sleep around here."

Sonja caught her sarcasm. "I haven't scored too many points with you folks, have I? I'm probably on Ted's hit list, too. Time to travel on, I guess. I was really beginning to enjoy him, too. Great dancer."

Thelma gave the bread she was kneading an extra punch and pursed her lips. She didn't dare comment on that one but instead said, "A girl as pretty as you must have the men lined up around the block."

"Bor-ing. The country club is crawling with rich men—most of which I've dated. One look and they come running. I must admit this backwoods detour has had a couple of challenging prospects. But then Amy knows all about that, doesn't she?"

Before Thelma could comment, the other three came out of Henry's office and into the kitchen.

Amy looked at Sonja who was finishing her second cup of coffee. "I've talked to Ted and he'll be down in about fifteen minutes to take you to the marina."

"So he isn't angry with me then?"

"From what I gathered last night, he wasn't angry with you at all. More concerned than anything else."

"He's such a dear. I'm surprised you haven't noticed that quality in him, Amy. You've known him longer than I. But then, you've set your sights higher, haven't you?"

Sonja's last remark stung but she refused to bite.

"Come along, dear," Elaine patted her daughter's shoulder. "We still have things to pack."

Chapter Twenty-six

The Newmans returned to their cottage, Thelma began greasing bread pans, and Amy went back into the office. She'd left Lyle's check on the desk and she wanted to put it in the vault. As the door swung open, an official looking paper slid to the floor. Amy picked it up and noticed it was the standard purchase agreement form used when a piece of property changed hands.

"Oh, no," she said aloud, "Daddy, you forgot this!"

Her eyes scanned the black print and froze on the purchaser's signature. There in bold letters was the name Matthew Monroe! Not Canadian Uranium as she expected.

"Matt! What's his name doing here? There has to be a mistake!"

Amy scrutinized every word of the contract. It was spelled out in plain English; Matt agreed to buy Pine Lake Lodge. The paper in her hand began to shake and her legs felt weak. She leaned against the desk to keep her knees from buckling. Why hadn't she been told? Why was her father meeting with Tom Evans today? And most important, why was Matt interested in the lodge?

The momentary relief Amy felt from the reprieve of knowing the mining company would have to look elsewhere, soon turned to anger and a nauseous feeling grew in the pit of her stomach. It occurred to her that Matt's tenderness might have been nothing more than a sham to win her over to his side once the deal went through. The nerve of that man!

"Thelma," Amy ran into the kitchen waving the document in the air. "Do you know anything about this?"

"Good heavens, girl, what's gotten into you? You look fit to be tied!"

"Read this. I found it in the vault."

Thelma wiped her hands on her apron before picking up the paper. As she read, her breath quickened and her mouth widened.

"Well, this certainly sheds new light on things, doesn't it? Believe me, Amy, this is the first I knew of it. What on earth would Matt want with a place this size?"

"It beats me, but I intend to find out. It's not like Daddy to keep something like this from me."

Ted's boat came into view so Amy dropped the subject.

"We'll talk later. I'd better see that the Newmans get off all right. Sure don't want Sonja left behind!"

"Calm down. She'll soon be gone."

"True, but I have another score to settle." Amy folded the contract and placed it in her shirt pocket.

Ted was busy loading luggage into his boat when Amy stepped onto the dock. "For someone who was up most of the night, you look lively today." She handed him a cooler.

"Morning. Listen, I'm sorry about last night. Didn't mean to drag you out of bed. Don't suppose I'll ever live that one down, eh? Sonja give you any trouble?"

"Slept like a baby all the way home. Don't feel bad.

Lyle says you aren't the first to bring her home inebriated."

"She kept the bartender busy. No doubt about that."

Behind them a screen door opened and Lyle appeared with a couple of coats slung over his arm. "We're almost ready, Ted. The girls will be along shortly."

"Lyle, I apologize for the worry I put you and Elaine through last night. I had no idea the night would turn out like it did."

"Say no more, son. It's clear who was at fault. Maybe someday Sonja will see how irresponsible she is and grow up."

A familiar voice called out, "Did I hear my name?"

She bounced down the steps and ran toward Ted. Before he knew it, she planted a kiss on his lips, cooing, "Thanks for taking care of me last night. I had a great time."

Ted's face flushed, but he maintained his sense of humor, "I'm surprised you remembered."

Sonja was speechless. Leave it to Ted to get the last word. He jumped in the boat and started the motor.

Elaine and Lyle warmly embraced Amy as they said their farewells, while Sonja, already seated, gave no more than a half-hearted wave. Amy watched until the boat was out of sight then turning from the lake, looked at Matt's cottage. The door was closed and a brief look at the dock showed that his boat was missing.

Amy stomped her foot on the dock!   "Rats!"   she muttered. "He would have to be gone."

She'd taken a few steps toward the empty cottage to strip the linen when she heard Thelma call, "Amy, telephone. Jamie's wife."

Rushing up the trail, she wondered, "What does she want so early?"

"Amy," the voice was anxious. "It's Karen. I need your help. I've gone into labor and Jamie's not here. Took a group on an overnight trip. My sister's kids are sick and

Mom fell last week and sprained her ankle. I'm desperate. I need you to watch the twins. Please."

"Karen, calm down. I'll be right over. Have your bag packed and ready to go the second I get there, okay? Bye. Karen's in labor. I have to go. Jamie's gone—heaven knows where and she needs me to watch the twins!"

"Get a move on, Amy. Babies come on their own schedule."

Amy raced up the stairs, threw a change of clothes and some toiletries into an overnight bag and was out the door shouting over her shoulder, "Could be a couple days before I'm back. Say a prayer this baby stays put 'til I get Karen to the doctor."

A mile from the marina, Amy spotted a boat anchored in a small bay. The lone occupant sat with one leg propped up on the gunnel, a fishing rod in his right hand, and the brim of his baseball cap pulled down over his eyes. Apparently Matt was catching a few winks after last night's ordeal. The temptation to stop and get to the bottom of her morning's discovery was almost more than she could stand. But, time was not on her side; she had to go.

No one was around the marina to delay her, so Amy secured her boat, ran to her car, unlocked the door, and sped out of the parking lot, throwing bits of gravel in all directions for the next three miles.

She gave a sigh of relief when she saw her passengers waiting on the porch. From the look on Karen's face there wasn't time to turn off the engine.

"Hope you called Dr. Willis."

"Yep. He's waiting for me. Told me to time my contractions."

"And how close are they?"

"About every five to seven minutes. When's the last time you delivered a baby, Amy?" Karen chuckled through her discomfort.

"That's not one bit funny. We're burning rubber,

Honey. Buckle up, boys."

Amy left a choking cloud of dust behind her Saturn as she drove the six miles to the small country hospital. The staff wasted no time in getting Karen into the delivery room so Amy took the boys into the waiting area.

The twins insisted on Amy reading to them and they were on the sixth book when Dr. Willis announced that the boys had a new baby brother. Mother and son were fine. After a morning filled with anxiety and tension, the news was welcome relief.

By the time Amy got Brett and Stephen home, they were ready for their afternoon nap. She used the break to call relatives and give them the news. Of course there were the usual questions. How much does he weigh? How long was Karen in labor? And who does he look like? As a result, it was late afternoon before Amy had a chance to call home. Thelma, true to form, was full of questions, too. Did Karen have any problems? When will Jamie be home, and last but not least, how was she coping with two three-year olds? Finally, Thelma stopped her interrogation long enough to allow Amy to ask, "Is Daddy home yet?"

"Told me not to expect him before dark. You know the lawyer's office is seventy miles one way and Henry's not one to speed. He intended to visit your mom, too. Oh, I almost forgot. Matt came in with an eight-pound pickerel! Sure was proud of it! Sounded disappointed when I told him you wouldn't be back tonight."

"How's that?"

"He just kind of muttered something like, "I'll have to wait 'til next time."

"Next time. It doesn't make any sense to me. I don't have a clue what he meant."

The sounds of squabbling interrupted Amy's conversation. "Gotta go. The boys are up. Talk to you tomorrow. Bye"

The active play and imagination of toddlers was what

Amy needed to distract her from her own tangled thoughts. Every time she pondered Matt's comment, one of the boys claimed her attention. If it wasn't a cookie they wanted, then it was a favorite game they insisted she play with them. The time passed quickly and before she knew it, everyone was settling down for the night. Unbuttoning her shirt, she noticed the purchase agreement still folded and tucked in the pocket where she'd put it earlier this morning. Amy resolved that another day would not pass without her finding out the truth. Who intended to buy Pine Lake Lodge? Canadian Uranium or Matthew Monroe?

Chapter Twenty-seven

"Amy, get up! Get up!" Two little boys jumped on her bed giggling and squealing. "Time to play. You promised we could take our trucks down to the beach."

"Whoa, guys." She stole a look at her watch and saw that it was only seven a.m. "It's way too early! I'm still half asleep. Look at my sleepy eyes."

"We'll wake you up," volunteered Stephen, rollicking over her stomach, while Brett proceeded to tickle her ribs. For the next half hour, the bedclothes looked like they'd been caught in a whirlwind as the twins bounced and pranced all over the mattress. Finally, with his energy spent, Brett announced, "Hungry, Amy. Let's eat."

"Pancakes, please. With lots of syrup," his brother ordered.

While the boys ate their breakfast, Amy walked to the phone. She imagined Henry was draining his third cup of coffee and probably ready to head out the door to begin some project. She'd catch him before he got involved.

What was the truth? Who bought the lodge? She put the receiver to her ear and started to punch in her number when she realized there was no dial tone. Total silence!

"No, no, no," she slammed the receiver onto its cradle. "The line can't be dead—not today."

Her actions startled the twins and Stephen asked, "What's wrong? Are you mad?"

"Just at the phone, guys. I need to talk to your uncle Henry but I guess the lightening hit it again last night."

Amy sighed. There was no point in frustrating herself any further so she cleaned up the kitchen, washed up the boys and dressed them for the day. The energy of twin three-year-olds kept her focused on their every move.

Shortly after lunch, while putting Brett and Stephen down for their nap, she heard Jamie's voice calling out to Karen, "Hey, hon, I'm home."

Tip-toeing down the stairs, Amy hushed, "Shh, I just got the boys settled."

Jamie looked at her in surprise. "What are you doing here? Oh, no! She had the baby, didn't she? Dang! It wasn't due 'til next week."

Amy gave her cousin a hug. "Congratulations! Another boy! Everything's fine. Get on into town and see your new son."

"Thanks, Amy. We owe you." He was in his truck and on his way before the screen door slammed shut.

While preparing a macaroni casserole for supper, a thought came to Amy she hadn't even considered. How would her mother react to the sale of the lodge? Relief? Regret?

Amy felt certain her father told her the truth yesterday.

"In fact," Amy mused, "she probably knows more about the situation than I do. Maybe this will be the turning point that puts her on a road to recovery."

Since communication to the lodge was cut off, Amy was anxious to return, so she left as soon as Jamie drove into the driveway. At the marina, Ted filled up the Evinrude's gas tank and was ready to untie her boat when he said,

"Hey! Have you talked to anyone at the lodge today?"

"Last night's storm must have knocked out the line again. Couldn't get a dial tone all day. Why?"

"Matt caught a whopper of a pickerel! He sure was proud of it. He's fished so hard this summer it was good to see him finally land something worthwhile."

"Thelma told me about it yesterday. I'll see it when I get home."

"Afraid not, Amy."

"What do you mean? Did he release it?"

"No. He froze it and took it back to Ohio."

"You mean he's gone!" Amy scanned the parking lot for his car.

"Left about noon. But then I guess you wouldn't know since you spent the night at Jamie's. He didn't say why he had to leave, but he told me he'd be seeing me again."

"When?"

"I didn't ask. Say, what's going on? You look upset."

"Just some unfinished business." She was close to tears.

"You need to talk?"

"Not 'til I get some facts straight. Right now I've got more questions than answers. Shove me off, Ted, I need to talk to my father."

Chapter Twenty-eight

The evening breeze was cooler now that summer was coming to an end, and she shivered as the boat gained speed. Learning that Matt was gone left Amy with an emptiness she couldn't explain. It wasn't the same feeling she'd experienced when her mother left the lodge. Yes, she'd missed her, but Amy knew she could visit at any time. No, this was a different kind of emptiness. It felt as though Matt had physically taken a part of her with him. The earlier anticipation of meeting him suddenly fell flat and her shoulders drooped in disappointment.

As Amy drew closer to the lodge, her eyes followed the familiar path to Matt's cottage. No fishing rods leaned against the porch railing, no lights flickered inside, and no boat was tied to the dock. With a heavy heart, Amy tied her own craft and walked toward the lodge.

Thelma was mashing potatoes when she opened the kitchen door and the smell of roast beef permeated the air.

"Welcome home. We waited until this minute to eat.

Henry's starving so I told him we'd go ahead and I'd save a plate for you. Thought you said to expect you about four."

"You're right, I told you yesterday I'd be home late afternoon, but I knew Jamie was anxious to see Karen and the baby, so I stayed with the twins a couple hours longer than I planned."

"Why didn't you call?"

"Tried to, but their phone's out again. Seems like every time there's a storm they lose it for awhile."

"Nonsense isn't it?"

"I got a surprise at the marina. Ted tells me Matt left this morning. Any clue why he left so suddenly?"

"Didn't tell me, Amy. I know you're disappointed you didn't get a chance to talk to him. Oh, I almost forgot." Thelma dug into her apron pocket and pulled out an envelope. "He asked me to give you this."

Amy's fingers shook as she tore at its contents. The message was short. "Amy, I have to leave today. Your father can explain. We have to talk. I'll be back. Matt."

She read it again, this time the words tumbled from her lips in a whisper and her eyes glistened.

"Amy, sounds to me like your going to see him again."

At the sound of the women's voices, Henry emerged from his office and gave his daughter a kiss on the forehead.

"Hi, sweetheart. Looks like the boys did you in!"

Amy forced a smile. "I survived. Daddy, why didn't you tell me? Why is Matt Monroe's name on this contract?" Her voice trembled as her hand pulled it from her shirt pocket.

Henry looked surprised. "So that's where it went. I've been looking high and low for it since I got back. Matt took his copy with him."

"Why Matt? What happened to Canadian Uranium?" She was teetering on impatience.

"Amy, however you found out about this, I'm sorry.

We didn't intend to shut you out. Let me explain."

"So it's true?" She was still in denial. "Yes, yes. I want to know everything."

Henry took a deep breath and started, "I told you before that Matt's father is a doctor. He specializes in handicapped cases. Matt tells me that ever since he came home with his leg injury, his dad wants to help veterans. Dr. Monroe has been looking for a place large enough to be used as a summer retreat for patients. Some can't afford to take a regular vacation and most places aren't equipped for them. It'll be along the lines of those camps for kids with cancer."

"But our lodge isn't prepared to handle wheelchairs and walkers."

"True, not yet, so changes have to be made and Matt has asked me to stay on as manager. We'll build boardwalks along the trails and doorways have to be widened. There's a lot we can do if we put our heads together to help these folks."

Amy was not finished. "I still don't understand why either of you didn't tell me what was going on."

"Honey," Henry's voice softened, "we both knew how you felt about selling the lodge to the mining company. Matt got the final go-ahead only two nights ago. If it didn't go through, we didn't want you disappointed."

"Then why was it necessary to go to the lawyer's office yesterday with Bob Evans?"

"I felt I had an obligation to meet with Bob and explain why I decided to decline the company's offer. We talked it over at his motel, and then I went on to the lawyer's myself. Had to get the paperwork rolling for Matt. I have to admit, it felt good knowing a mining company wouldn't be turning this place into a base camp."

"Amen," Amy agreed.

"I feel good about Matt's deal, though. Seems right. He'll make it work; I can tell by his determination. It's more than a job to him—it's a dream. Great guy!"

"I don't think you'll argue with that, will you?" Thelma teased giving Amy's shoulder an affectionate hug.

The blush on Amy's cheeks confirmed Henry's affirmation and deepened as he continued, "Matt felt badly that he missed seeing you, Amy. I know he wanted to explain this to you himself. His dad called this morning and asked him to get this settled immediately. There's legal work that has to be done, especially since Matt's not a resident, and they don't want to waste any time. He left a binder so we know he's serious."

"Well, I see you've left the best for last," chuckled Thelma.

"Did I leave something out?" quizzed Henry.

Thelma straightened her stand and a smile lit her face. "I'm to be the head cook in this new venture. Matt asked me to return next spring. They plan to have a common dining room."

"That's wonderful!" It was Amy's turn to hug her friend. "I knew your cooking would get through to him. But I don't understand. You told me you knew nothing about Matt's name on the purchase agreement. When did he ask you?"

"Your father told me the whole story when he got home last night. Then Matt talked to me this morning before he left."

Henry became serious. "We've been going on about our part in this project, but how do you feel, Amy?"

"Relieved and overwhelmed to be honest. A lot has happened in the last two days. Matt's idea is exciting! It'll be a challenge but I know you're up to it. You're happy, aren't you? I can see that sparkle back in your eyes!" Amy gave him a hug before asking, "And what was mom's reaction? You did tell her, didn't you?"

"I did. Seemed like a bitter-sweet response. I could see the relief in her voice but I saw sadness in her eyes, too.

We've been partners a long time in this business. She said she'd miss the lake but she doesn't want any part of Matt's plans. Too many memories. She's content to come back to our house in town. It won't be any problem for me working from there."

"Any idea when she'll be home?"

"The doctors have to make that call, but it sure would be nice if it were sooner than later. I've missed her."

"I know you have," said Amy, her eyes misting. For the first time in her life she knew how it felt to miss someone so much her heart ached to be with him.

*   *   *

While the two women cleaned up the supper dishes, Amy was unusually quiet. She went through the mechanical motions of her task but her mind appeared to be somewhere else. Thelma broke the silence.

"Amy, you don't seem as happy as I thought you'd be knowing Matt has rescued Pine Lake Lodge. Now, I know you didn't want Canadian Uranium hanging its shingle here. What's up?" She stopped scrubbing the potato pot, looked at Amy and waited for an answer.

Amy took a deep breath before beginning, "I'm relieved that this place won't be crawling with miners and that daddy no longer has to shoulder a financial burden. He won't have to leave the home he put his heart and soul into for over thirty-five years. But he doesn't need me anymore. I can't stay." Amy's voice broke, "Especially, if Matt comes back married."

"Hearsay, my girl! Nothing but hearsay!" Thelma plopped the pot into the rinse sink so hard she sent water flying in all directions.

"I guess we'll know when he gets back, won't we? When will that be, Thelma? Did he tell you?"

"He didn't know for sure. I suppose it's anybody's guess. Legal matters take their time and there may be extra red tape on this deal, seeing how it's an American buying

151

this place. Oh, he mentioned something about going to Germany before the end of the month, too."

"Germany! Like for a honeymoon, maybe? Thelma, you know patience isn't one of my virtues, so I'm giving you fair warning. It could be a long month. Lord knows when I'll get to have my little chat with him."

Chapter Twenty-nine

There was no point in putting the job off any longer. The cottage Matt had occupied only three days ago needed to be cleaned. Once a guest vacated, then the place was scrubbed and polished to make ready for the next. No matter who owned the lodge, Amy would make sure each cottage was spotlessly clean.

Physically, Amy knew Matt wasn't there, but the moment she opened the door, it was like he never left. His presence was everywhere: a sports magazine lay on the coffee table, an odd sock attached itself to the end of the broom as Amy swept under the bed, and the pillowcases smelled of his after shave. Each little reminder made her aware of how much she missed him. He'd left memories she'd always treasure and a void only he could fill.

Completing her task, Amy sat on the porch. She leaned back against the wall and closed her eyes. Sounds of lapping waves and chirping birds broke the silence. Although the sun's rays were weakening, they still felt good on her weary body. Her mind wandered to the beginning of summer and her first impression of Matt. Tainted by Eric's arrogance, she realized there had been times she'd been defensive. But in all honesty, he'd provoked her, too. She wondered if events during the past two months had chiseled away the past hurt he'd been through to reveal the warm, understanding man who captured her heart? She hoped if nothing else, he'd found the peace he was looking for.

As the days moved forward, Amy realized they would have to sort out thirty-five years of accumulation. Some things would stay but there were personal items that needed to go to the house in town. She dreaded the thought. Her mother had always accused her father of being a pack rat and the truth was all around them. Henry's trips to the local dump usually brought back as much as he took.

"Look," he'd say, "someone threw out this perfectly good shovel. All I have to do is put a new handle on it."

For the next two weeks, Amy sorted, packed, and labeled boxes from morning until late afternoon. It was good physical and mental therapy. Busy hands kept her mind from wandering across the U.S./Canadian border.

Summer was on the wane and fall showed signs of eagerly awaiting its debut. Squirrels stuffed acorns and hazel nuts into their mouths until their cheeks stretched to the limit. The last of the garden vegetables looked scrumptious in the clear preserving jars and the evening temperature dropped another few degrees.

The first frost nipped the roses in the front yard leaving their pastel petals limp and lifeless. The new autumn foliage, however, was stunning. The forest was ablaze with hues of orange, gold, and crimson. All too soon, though, Amy knew they would hold center stage no longer and drop silently from their lofty perch to the earth below.

A sense of melancholy always haunted Amy at this time of year. She determined it was the fact that the excitement of the summer days was over and everything around her was preparing for the long winter months ahead. This year, the ache in her heart intensified this mood. Each day that went by with no word from Matt worked on her mind until she was convinced they'd never see him again. Why hadn't he called or written? Surely he and his father hadn't changed their minds. To have Matt renege on this deal with her father was unthinkable!

Evenings were the worst for Amy. She managed to keep busy during the day, but at night she felt at loose ends. On one such evening, as she tried to focus on a novel her attention was interrupted by the phone. Each time this happened, her heart beat quickened. Could it be Matt calling at last?

"Hello."

"Amy, it's Karen."

"Is everything all right?" She tried not to show her disappointment.

"Oh, we're fine. The baby is gaining weight every day." There was a pause before Karen continued. "I have to tell you something and I hope you won't be upset."

"Upset? What are you talking about?"

"Well, it happened this way." Karen chose to give all the details. "An envelope addressed to you was put in our mail by mistake. You know how they're always getting our mail mixed up 'cause of the same last name."

"Yeah," Amy said, "what's the big deal? I'll come over in the morning and get it."

"I'm afraid you can't do that."

"Why not?"

"There isn't any envelope. I had it on the cupboard ready to return to you, and sometime during the day, one of the twins got hold of it and cut it into tiny pieces. I'm really sorry, Amy."

"Oh, Karen, it's probably a bill. Don't worry; I'll get another one next month."

"It wasn't a bill. It was a personal letter. The only part

155

I managed to salvage was the return address."

"Oh," Amy showed some concern. "Who was it from?"

"Do you know a Matt Monroe?"

Amy thought her heart had stopped beating. Finally, after waiting in agony to hear from Matt, she received a letter she'd never be able to read.

"Yes," her answer was faint. "Karen, do you still have the pieces? Could I put them back together?"

"Gee, he made quite a mess of the paper. I just threw it into the garbage. Important letter, eh? I just feel rotten."

"Hey, kids will be kids. Thanks for letting me know."

Amy hung up the receiver in a trance. She was still trying to comprehend the circumstances when Thelma came in.

"Good heavens, girl! Who was on that phone? You look stunned."

"Thelma, sit down. You're not going to believe this."

Amy related her dilemma. "Who knows what was in that letter? I'm so frustrated I don't know what to do!"

"Before you get yourself all worked up, why don't you take things in your own hands and call Matt. Tell him what happened. At least you'd have satisfaction, no matter what he says."

"You mean now, tonight?"

"There's no time like the present. His number must be in your father's office somewhere."

"You're right! He should've written it in the guest book when he left."

Frantically searching under a stack of paperwork, Amy located the book and leafed through the pages until she found his name. Trembling fingers dialed the number then waited as the phone rang, once, twice, three times. On the fourth ring, a familiar voice informed her that Matt Monroe was not in at the present, but if she cared to leave a message after the beep, he'd get back to her.

Thelma heard the slam of the receiver from where she was sitting in the living room, followed by Amy's frustration! "If he thinks I'm going to pour my heart out to an answering machine, he's crazy!"

Walking back to join Thelma, her report was simple, "He's not home."

Chapter Thirty

The constant buzz of the alarm clock in Amy's ears was a cruel reminder that there was no time to lounge in bed. Work was the only thing on her agenda and the ache in her back reinforced that reality. The last box she picked up yesterday was heavier than she thought and now her muscles were letting her know. Enough is enough!

As usual, Thelma had breakfast well under way when she entered the kitchen.

"I'm cooking pancakes and eggs for you this morning, young lady."

"Thelma, you know I never have anything more than toast and cereal. What's the big deal?"

"You're going to need it for energy."

"Am I looking anemic?" Amy teased.

"Don't laugh, you may be by the time you're finished helping your father."

"Thelma, I'm going to town to run errands today and I've done enough of that this summer."

"From what I hear, the plans have changed."

"Oh no," Amy sighed, "you mean he wants me to help him scrub boats. Then of course we have to put them away today?"

A smirk crossed Thelma's face. "You wish! How 'bout cleaning out the storage shed? The one that hasn't been touched by human hands in fifteen years!"

Amy grimaced, "You've got to be kidding! How could a father do that to his only daughter? Do you realize once I get in the middle of that mess, I may not be seen for a week!"

Thelma couldn't pass on an opportunity to needle Amy further. "Look at it this way; you may find antiques that are worth a fortune. Listen, I know folks who'd sell their soul to be in your shoes today."

"Yes, but where are they when you need them? Are you positive Daddy doesn't want me to go to town?"

"I'm afraid Thelma's right." Henry emerged from his office with his empty coffee cup in hand. "I've been puttin' it off and puttin' it off. Can't let another day go by without digging into that mess."

"You know I'm teasing you. Who knows, we may find the family jewels! Go ahead. I'll be with you as soon as I finish these pancakes."

A few hours into the job and Amy was grateful for the generous breakfast Thelma insisted she eat. She reached, she bent, she climbed all over the paraphernalia Henry had collected over the years. Every now and then she'd find a remnant of her childhood. A pair of red rubber boots reminded her of the many times she walked in the water along the shoreline catching leopard frogs to sell as bait.

Hanging on a peg was a large two-man, snag-toothed saw, worn rusty with age. How many logs had been hewn and shaped by its cutting blade? The list of items was endless and Amy knew she couldn't afford the time to reminisce over each one. As she looked at the pile of junk she mentally earmarked 'dump-final destination', she realized they were making progress. The bottom of the shed was clean. Now, the attic remained.

After a short break for lunch, Amy grabbed her radio and returned to her task. Henry, sidetracked by a broken faucet, left her on her own. Listening to a "Golden Oldie" station was exactly what she needed to renew her enthusiasm. Each time she climbed onto the rafters, to pull down some box or basket, she'd bump her head and before long her hair was matted with dust and cobwebs.

Her clothes reeked of mildew, her body of sweat, and grease smudges covered her arms, hands, and one cheek.

The job was almost completed when over the blasting radio she heard someone call her name. It wasn't Thelma; it wasn't Henry; it was Matt! Was she imagining she'd heard his voice? It seemed real. Amy peeked through the small hole in the floor that concealed the pull-down ladder.

Her mind was not playing tricks on her. There he was standing at the door of the shed handsome, muscular, and desirable. Panic sent blood rushing to her head, and all she could think of was, *I can't let him see me like this!*

"Amy, I know you're up there. Turn the radio off."

A push of the button brought silence.

"Now climb down the ladder or I'm coming up to get you. Stiff leg or not."

Knowing his determination, Amy took his threat seriously but she had to buy time.

"Where did you come from? I didn't hear any boat."

"I guess you didn't with Elvis serenading you up there. C'mon now, my dad's waiting to meet the girl I intend to marry."

"What?" Intend to what?" For a second Amy thought the loud music had damaged her hearing.

"Marry—as in man and wife. I already have your father's blessing."

"I don't believe you! Daddy would've told me."

"Sworn to secrecy, honey. But then didn't you read it in the purchase contract? The small print. Always read the small print. Seller agrees to give his daughter in marriage to the buyer—that's me."

Amy peeked down once more and saw the look of amusement on Matt's face as he continued, "I'm going to count to five, so you'd better start down."

He was already on three when Thelma came running up to him panting and spurting out the words, "Matt, your mom's on the phone. Take it in Henry's office."

"Amy," he shouted, "you owe my mom one. Wait 'til I tell her." Matt headed toward the office and Thelma peered up the ladder.

Sizing up the situation, she commanded, "Get out of here and into the shower, pronto, girl. You're a mess!"

Amy slid down the ladder and was almost in the kitchen when she turned back to Thelma and with tears smudging the dust on her cheeks said, "He asked me to marry him—well, kind of!"

Chapter Thirty-one

The transformation took less than an hour. A hot shower dissolved the sweaty dirt and grime from Amy's tanned, shapely body, an herbal essence shampoo washed the cobwebs from auburn hair that bounced and danced to the hum of a hair dryer, and finger nails glistened from a fresh coat of polish. Her lips and cheeks already pink from excitement, needed little make-up. She dressed in pressed denims and a soft rose-colored sweater that clung to her in all the right places. One glance in the mirror confirmed the improvement.

Ted was in the kitchen talking to Thelma as Amy skipped down the steps. He stopped in mid-sentence and said, "Brought ya someone special. Told you he'd be back."

"But you could've given me fair warning, Ted. He almost caught me looking like somethin' the cat dragged in!"

"We did call, but the line was busy. Matt didn't want to wait around, so you can blame him. Seemed pretty impatient to get back here."

"My fault you couldn't get through, Ted," Thelma confessed. "You know that sister of mine when we get to yakin'"

"Looks to me like you got your act together just fine, Amy." Ted nodded in approval. "Oh, before I forget, your dad says the beds in cabin eight need to be made up. Hop to it, girl. The new owner's here—no slacking off!"

Normally, this chore would have been done before the guests arrived, but since she'd had no advance notice, she piled the sheets and pillowcases on her arm and started down the trail. She was almost at the cottage when she came face to face with her father and a gray-haired man she guessed to be in his sixties. He bore a striking resemblance to Matt.

"Amy, this is Matt's father, Bob."

"A pleasure to meet you, Amy. Now I understand my son's itching to get back up here; and, I suspect it had nothing to do with the fishing. I feel as though I know you already. Matt's told me a lot."

Amy felt her cheeks burning but she also saw the look of approval in Bob's eyes as she shook his hand and said, "Welcome to Canada. And to your new home."

"Your dad's taking me on the tour now. From the little I've seen, I'm more than impressed. Good thing I insisted Matt take a vacation this summer." He smiled as he continued, "Say, I'm holding you up and there's someone in cabin eight who can't wait to see you. We'll talk more later."

Climbing the porch steps, Amy felt the burdens of the last month dissipate like the morning frost. She bounced up the steps and called through the screen door, "I'm here to officially welcome the new owner of Pine Lake Lodge. My apologies from the gal in the attic. She really needs to learn some manners."

At the sound of her voice, Matt lay down the fishing

rod he'd been assembling and opened the door. A mischievous smile lit his face. "No problem. You look a lot prettier than she did anyway."

For a second, time stood still; their eyes locked together. Amy searched for an answer. Does he truly love me? Matt took the first step toward her, reached for the linens and tossed them onto the sofa. His hands cupped her shoulders and instantly their bodies united. The softness of her body and the scent of freshly scrubbed skin were intoxicating. A groan of satisfaction caught in Matt's throat before he murmured, "I've missed you so much these past few weeks!"

"I've missed you, too! I thought you weren't coming back. Then your letter was destroyed. Did Daddy tell you what happened?"

Matt chuckled, "Never was much of a letter writer, but I wanted you to know I was in Germany. Dad needed me to check out a piece of therapy equipment he ordered for the clinic. I would've called but with the time difference I thought a letter was better. Besides, I needed to express some feelings to you on paper."

Their lips barely touched but Amy drew back and looked into Matt's puzzled face. "I have to know something. Who is Barbara Anderson?" She waited almost breathless.

"My dad's lawyer. She's known me since I was a kid. She called the night we were all having dinner at the lodge."

Amy gasped. "But Sonja led me to believe she was your…"

"Sonja told you I was in love with someone at home, didn't she? Well, I straightened her out the morning she left."

Tears glistened in Amy's eyes as she lowered her head and said, "I'm so embarrassed, Matt. I bought her story, hook, line, and sinker. She's so convincing."

Matt's hands framed her face and he tilted her chin upward before saying, "So that's why I got the cold shoulder, huh?"

Amy nodded.

"Listen to me. I knew I was falling in love with you that night on the beach. I walked away because I didn't know how to respond. It wasn't supposed to happen. After my divorce, I decided no woman would ever have a place in my heart again. I came to Canada to fish—nothing more. Day by day, you changed all that. Believe me, I love you. I want to spend the rest of my life with you."

"Matt," was all he would let her say before his lips kissed her long, hard, and with a pent-up passion they both knew could no longer be contained.

Finally, gasping for breath, Amy poured out the words held captive all summer. "I love you, too—so very much!"

Matt buried his face in the warmth of her neck, then spread butterfly kisses from her ear to her cheek to her forehead, drawing her yielding body closer with each one.

"Then I take it you have no objection to the small print in the contract I mentioned earlier?" The amused look on his face spoke of love.

"Well, now, why don't you explain it to me again without all that legal talk?"

"Plain and simple, will you marry me, Amy?"

She looked into his eyes, strong but sensitive, pressed her lips against his, and gave him her answer.

"Yes, oh, yes! I'll marry you."

Matt's arms gathered her closer and once again his kiss sent a delicious warmth racing through her body.

Destiny turned her life upside down and she tingled with excitement at what the future might hold for them. This man—-this summer guest turned out to be so much more. She couldn't wait to begin a life with him.

The End